Anthony Gilbert and The Murder Room

>>> This title is part of The Murder Room, our series dedicated to making available out-of-print or hard-to-find titles by classic crime writers.

Crime fiction has always held up a mirror to society. The Victorians were fascinated by sensational murder and the emerging science of detection; now we are obsessed with the forensic detail of violent death. And no other genre has so captivated and enthralled readers.

Vast troves of classic crime writing have for a long time been unavailable to all but the most dedicated frequenters of second-hand bookshops. The advent of digital publishing means that we are now able to bring you the backlists of a huge range of titles by classic and contemporary crime writers, some of which have been out of print for decades.

From the genteel amateur private eyes of the Golden Age and the femmes fatales of pulp fiction, to the morally ambiguous hard-boiled detectives of mid twentieth-century America and their descendants who walk our twenty-first century streets, The Murder Room has it all. **>>>**

The Murder Room
Where Criminal Minds Meet

themurderroom.com

Anthony Gilbert (1899–1973)

Anthony Gilbert was the pen name of Lucy Beatrice Malleson. Born in London, she spent all her life there, and her affection for the city is clear from the strong sense of character and place in evidence in her work. She published 69 crime novels, 51 of which featured her best known character, Arthur Crook, a vulgar London lawyer totally (and deliberately) unlike the aristocratic detectives, such as Lord Peter Wimsey, who dominated the mystery field at the time. She also wrote more than 25 radio plays, which were broadcast in Great Britain and overseas. Her thriller *The Woman in Red* (1941) was broadcast in the United States by CBS and made into a film in 1945 under the title *My Name is Julia Ross*. She was an early member of the British Detection Club, which, along with Dorothy L. Sayers, she prevented from disintegrating during World War II. Malleson published her autobiography, *Three-a-Penny*, in 1940, and wrote numerous short stories, which were published in several anthologies and in such periodicals as *Ellery Queen's Mystery Magazine* and *The Saint*. The short story 'You Can't Hang Twice' received a Queens award in 1946. She never married, and evidence of her feminism is elegantly expressed in much of her work.

By Anthony Gilbert

Scott Egerton series

Tragedy at Freyne (1927)

The Murder of Mrs
  Davenport (1928)

Death at Four Corners (1929)

The Mystery of the Open
  Window (1929)

The Night of the Fog (1930)

The Body on the Beam (1932)

The Long Shadow (1932)

The Musical Comedy
  Crime (1933)

An Old Lady Dies (1934)

The Man Who Was Too
  Clever (1935)

**Mr Crook Murder
  Mystery series**

Murder by Experts (1936)

The Man Who Wasn't
  There (1937)

Murder Has No Tongue (1937)

Treason in My Breast (1938)

The Bell of Death (1939)

Dear Dead Woman (1940)
  aka *Death Takes a Redhead*

The Vanishing Corpse (1941)
  aka *She Vanished in the Dawn*

The Woman in Red (1941)
  aka *The Mystery of the
  Woman in Red*

Death in the Blackout (1942)
  aka *The Case of the Tea-
  Cosy's Aunt*

Something Nasty in the
  Woodshed (1942)
  aka *Mystery in the Woodshed*

The Mouse Who Wouldn't
  Play Ball (1943)
  aka *30 Days to Live*

He Came by Night (1944)
  aka *Death at the Door*

The Scarlet Button (1944)
  aka *Murder Is Cheap*

A Spy for Mr Crook (1944)

The Black Stage (1945)
  aka *Murder Cheats the Bride*

Don't Open the Door (1945)
  aka *Death Lifts the Latch*

Lift Up the Lid (1945)
  aka *The Innocent Bottle*

The Spinster's Secret (1946)
  aka *By Hook or by Crook*

Death in the Wrong Room
  (1947)

Die in the Dark (1947)
  aka *The Missing Widow*

Death Knocks Three Times
  (1949)

Murder Comes Home (1950)

A Nice Cup of Tea (1950)
  aka *The Wrong Body*

Lady-Killer (1951)

Miss Pinnegar Disappears (1952)
 aka *A Case for Mr Crook*

Footsteps Behind Me (1953)
 aka *Black Death*

Snake in the Grass (1954)
 aka *Death Won't Wait*

Is She Dead Too? (1955)
 aka *A Question of Murder*

And Death Came Too (1956)

Riddle of a Lady (1956)

Give Death a Name (1957)

Death Against the Clock (1958)

Death Takes a Wife (1959)
 aka *Death Casts a Long Shadow*

Third Crime Lucky (1959)
 aka *Prelude to Murder*

Out for the Kill (1960)

She Shall Die (1961)
 aka *After the Verdict*

Uncertain Death (1961)

No Dust in the Attic (1962)

Ring for a Noose (1963)

The Fingerprint (1964)

The Voice (1964)
 aka *Knock, Knock! Who's There?*

Passenger to Nowhere (1965)

The Looking Glass Murder (1966)

The Visitor (1967)

Night Encounter (1968)
 aka *Murder Anonymous*

Missing from Her Home (1969)

Death Wears a Mask (1970)
 aka *Mr Crook Lifts the Mask*

Murder is a Waiting Game (1972)

Tenant for the Tomb (1971)

A Nice Little Killing (1974)

Standalone Novels

The Case Against Andrew Fane (1931)

Death in Fancy Dress (1933)

The Man in the Button Boots (1934)

Courtier to Death (1936)
 aka *The Dover Train Mystery*

The Clock in the Hatbox (1939)

Give Death a Name

Anthony Gilbert

An Orion book

Copyright © Lucy Beatrice Malleson 1957

The right of Lucy Beatrice Malleson to be identified as the author of this work has
been asserted in accordance with the Copyright, Designs and Patents Act 1988.

This edition published by
The Orion Publishing Group Ltd
Orion House
5 Upper St Martin's Lane
London WC2H 9EA

An Hachette UK company
A CIP catalogue record for this book is available from the British Library

ISBN 978 1 4719 1008 1

www.orionbooks.co.uk

To Dorothy
With gratitude
She will know why

In her dream she was sitting on a seat overlooking the sea; the spring afternoon was drawing to a close, a light mist was thickening over the water; before night it would have developed into fog. Round the lamps, that were already kindled, was that faint aura that betokens moisture in the atmosphere; behind her people were moving quickly, talking, saying it was time to be getting along. A young mother, with two children and a baby in a push-cart, went by, scolding one of the little boys for stroking a strange dog.

'It might bite you,' she said, 'and people can die of dog-bites.'

(She wanted to say, 'Only if the dog's mad', but she said nothing, because in dreams you never do the obvious thing.)

The little boy asked, 'What's die?' and his mother answered, rather crossly: 'Go away from me and Dad and Bert and Rosie. You wouldn't like that.'

'Go where?' asked the little boy.

'I know where you're going the minute you get home and that's bed,' retorted the overtaxed mother.

(She thought, 'I'll never speak to my children like that.')

Then the quartet had gone by, and two elderly women crossed in front of her, one saying, 'I couldn't believe it, dear. Marked down to six-and-eleven from four pounds. Oh no, it wasn't a mistake. I asked specially. It was just that it was a difficult colour to wear. Luckily I can wear anything. . . .'

Then they, too, had vanished and a young man lounged up, hands in pockets, leaning against the rail and staring out at the water. The gulls were coming inland—didn't they say that was a sign of bad weather? Three of them actually perched on the rail; the young man took his hands out of his pockets and clapped and they all went away. They flew so close she could see the red legs hanging down, their bright, predatory black eyes, almost feel the wind their wings made as they flashed off. The young man put his hands back in his pockets and strolled up to the seat where she sat.

'Waiting for someone, sunshine?'

She thought vaguely, again as you do in dreams, 'He can't be speaking to me. I don't know him.'

'Cat got your tongue?' suggested the young man, seating himself casually beside her. 'Wakey-wakey, sweetheart.'

She stood up abruptly, and walked over to the rail; she had a blue leather shoulder-bag that swung against her hip, and soft blue gloves that wrinkled over her wrists. She pulled them off and stuffed them into the pocket of the long blue coat. She half expected the young man to follow her, but he whistled and shrugged and went away, like the little family and the two women and the gulls, all going away from her. She turned and looked over her shoulder; behind her was a long row of shops, all the windows brilliantly lighted; between her and the shops the traffic moved, the green and white omnibuses, the cars, the delivery vans. A busy place . . . her thoughts stopped abruptly. In dreams places don't have names and this was a dream, so naturally she didn't know where she was.

'This,' she thought, desperately, 'is where I wake up.' She put out a hand, as if groping for an electric light switch, but it met only the air. The other hand was still clasped on the railing.

'Oh dear,' she told herself, 'I'm still asleep. But in a minute . . . ' It happened like that sometimes. You knew you were asleep, you knew this was unreality, yet it seemed more assured than truth. 'I am—I am——' for the moment she couldn't even remember who she was. She fought her way towards reality, but it was like fighting against a locked door. Turn the knob, push, then turn it the other way, now it's bound to open. And it doesn't. In spite of all your efforts, it stays locked, and you're by yourself in a dark room, which, being dark, is unfamiliar, you can't place it. Put out your hand, fumble for the light, but there's no light there. Try the other wall, and the result's the same. And you daren't leave go of the handle in case you can't find it again. So then you start panicking. Silly, isn't it, but dreams are like that.

Well, dreams were all very well, but this dream was becoming a nightmare. It was taking her towards something unknown, from which, perhaps, she wouldn't be able to return. But that's nonsense, nonsense. Sooner or later, you always come back. Only—suppose it's true, that there really is a place known as the Point of No Return? Suppose you got so lost in a dream you never found your way back?

She said aloud, 'But that's fantastic. I am—I am——'

With a sense of relief she felt the bag swing against her hip and snapped it open. That would tell her who she was. Her hand on the hasp, she came to a dead stop. Why on earth should she imagine she needed anything to reassure her on so elementary a point? She was—she was—odd not to be able to remember, except (she came back to the only reassuring argument) in dreams it did happen that way, of course it did. Why, sometimes, even after you'd waked up you lay puzzled, shocked even, before your own personality came back to you. Once she had dreamed she was going to marry an Arab— imagine it!—still, she remembered the dream now, which proved she hadn't really lost herself. Wait a minute, only a minute, and you'd be back in your own room, wherever that might be, laughing like anything at your own momentary panic in that instant before waking. Funny, someone *was* laughing. She looked round. A middle-aged woman was standing close by, watching her intently.

'Go away,' she thought, furiously. 'Go away. I hate being watched, I've always hated it.'

The woman came nearer. It wasn't she who was laughing, her face was grave, startled even. And there wasn't anyone else. Which meant—which meant—the laughter stopped as abruptly as it had begun.

'Are you feeling all right?' the woman asked.

'Of course.' (Don't panic.) 'I was waiting for someone, that's all, but I don't think I'll wait any longer. It's getting late— isn't it?'

3

Automatically she glanced at her wrist. Almost half past five.
'Yes,' said the woman in a soothing voice. 'I shouldn't wait
any longer. It's getting cold. I should go back, straight back.'
'Yes,' she agreed eagerly. 'That's what I'll do.'

She managed some sort of smile and turned and crossed the
road. She didn't look over her shoulder, she was afraid she'd
see the woman watching her. Walk calmly, glance in the shop
windows, then quickly take one of the turnings and be lost,
lost. Why, that's what I am, she discovered. Lost. Some of the
lights were beginning to go out in the shops as she passed
them, they were closing for the day. The feet of all those
around her were turning homewards. There was a purposeful-
ness about them, they were going home to father, husband,
child, to the solitary bed-sitter and high tea over a gas-ring,
or to a family, a sister, a dog even. They all had rendezvous
to keep, all but herself.

'But I have, too,' she insisted. 'I have, too. It's just that for
the moment I don't remember where.'

Remember? What? Why I'm here, how I came, where I'm
going. And then the truth she hadn't dared face till now
burst upon her. I don't know where I'm going because I don't
know who I am, who I am, who I am. The wind going shrilly
by echoed the words in her ear.

She looked up and saw the name *Beachampton Florist* over
a shop-front; a few doors farther on was *Beachampton Car
Service*. Beachampton. That rang a bell. It was a well-known
seaside resort, a holiday place. Yet she couldn't recollect ever
being here before. Still, you don't go to a strange place without
some reason. Someone is probably waiting for me now, saying,
'I wonder why she's late, if she missed the train, if she's had
an accident.' She stopped in front of a hat shop with a sheet
of plate-glass behind the models in the window. The light of
a street lamp illumined it and she saw a slender fair girl in a
long blue coat, a little blue cap, fair hair peeping out from
beneath it, an oval face—a pretty girl, you'd say, neat, attractive.
Hundreds of them about, of course, and nothing, so far as the
outward view went to distinguish this one from all the rest.
Blue eyes, a rather wide mouth faintly made up, a little colour

in the cheeks, tiny pearls in the small shapely ears. In towns, London, for example, you saw girls like that everywhere, straphanging in tubes, standing in bus queues, window-shopping, walking dogs in the park at week-ends. She looked down at her feet. Blue leather shoes, neat, with moderate heels, nylon stockings with straight seams, no runs, nothing twisted or awry. This girl hadn't been in an accident that might cause her to lose sight of her own identity even for five minutes. This girl had come here of her own free will—only—whence? Surely there would be something in the blue leather bag to answer her question. Because, if this really was a dream, then she was imprisoned in it. She was awake now, she felt sure of that, but somehow in sleep she had lost her way and needed a finger-post to guide her back.

Another face appeared in the glass beside hers, a woman in a red hat. The same woman? No, that one had worn brown. She moved, swerving violently, found herself by a tea-shop and went in. There weren't many people here at this hour, and there was no trouble about getting a table. A woman in a chintzy smock took her order, tea and toast, ordered without thinking. *(When did I eat last? I'm hungry, and yet I don't fancy food. But—I'm hungry.)* She opened the blue bag and noted the contents. Silver and copper in separate divisions, several pound notes in a zip pocket, a handkerchief of nice quality with the letter B embroidered in one corner, a half-crown book of stamps, partly used, but no wallet, as she had hoped, no wireless licence, no dog licence, no cheque-book, no Post Office Savings Bank book, no letters, no insurance card. She leaned back trying to look nonchalant as the waitress brought the tea and toast. The tea was hot and fragrant, the toast well-buttered.

'Cakes?' the woman inquired.

She supposed she said 'Yes,' because a minute later she returned with some excellent home-made cakes on a painted plate. The girl waited impatiently for her to go. Insurance card, that was the crux, that she must have. Everyone of her age had to have a card, by law. Quite what that age was she couldn't be certain. Twenty? Twenty-one? More? Never mind, she was exhausted, had had a shock of some kind that had momentarily

5

blocked memory. But take it easy, drink your tea, eat your toast, it'll all come back. It's like coming out of a dream, she repeated. Everything will soon be clear. There was no railway ticket in the bag, so probably this was where she lived. 'Someone's waiting for me, they'll think, How strange Mary—or Violet—or Jane—no, none of those because of the initial on the handkerchief—Barbara or Beatrice or Bianca—what other names began with B?—Berengaria, but that was the name of a ship, Blanche, only she felt sure she wasn't called Blanche—how strange that she doesn't come back.' She hadn't an umbrella or a raincoat, so clearly she had only just gone out for a walk; not to shop because she wasn't carrying any parcels.

'I went out,' she repeated, willing herself to remember. 'I went down to the front, but I didn't meet anyone. Or did I? Was there a scene of any kind? But in that case why am I alone? No. Then, I went to meet someone who didn't turn up, and the shock made me lose my memory.'

But that didn't make sense either. You didn't lose your memory because someone stood you up. You could be angry, incredulous, heartbroken, but you didn't instantly forget who you were. There was a newspaper lying discarded on a chair and she picked it up. People didn't look at you as if you were—odd—if you were reading a paper. A plane was overdue over the Atlantic, there was a provincial bus strike over new schedules, someone had held up a bank messenger, a TV personality had died and another one had got a divorce—the mixture as before and nothing whatever to give you a clue. Negative comfort, but comfort all the same, because at least there wasn't a paragraph to say the police were looking for a girl whose first name began with B, last seen wearing a blue coat and Juliet cap, carrying a shoulder-bag. . . . The police! She knew a sense of such revulsion that the paper shook in her hands and she laid it down. Why on earth should she feel like that at the mere thought of the police? Perhaps, as a child, her mother had said, 'If you're bad the police will come for you,' only people didn't say that any more, and anyway the modern child knew it had nothing to fear from the police. And yet—

that appalled sense of wanting to get inside something and pull down the lid at the mere thought of them. Pull down the lid? Ah, *The Wedding-Chest!* She had been told that story as a child, and it had haunted her for years. Oddly enough, the memory was reassuring now. Because, if she recalled even that reaction, surely the rest would follow. It was like being in a tunnel; you knew sooner or later you were bound to emerge into the light, only for some reason the train had come to a standstill. You heard other trains rumbling past, voices sounded in other carriages, but you were enclosed in this one like—a body in the grave? What a simile!

She was aware of the woman in the chintzy smock standing beside her table.

'Have you finished? We're shutting now.'

'Of course. I was day-dreaming. Just tea and toast.'

The woman's face changed, became hard and suspicious. 'Two cakes,' she said. 'You've had two cakes.'

Alarmed, the girl looked at the painted plate in the woman's hand. There were two gaps in the neatly arranged circle; she looked down at the plate in front of her. Cake crumbs without a doubt. So she'd eaten two cakes without realising it. Well, that wasn't surprising, considering the line her thoughts had taken.

'Oh dear,' she said, smiling apologetically. 'I must be wool-gathering. Yes, of course, two cakes. Delicious,' she added, trying to placate the enemy. The enemy? That was a silly expression, and yet not altogether without foundation. Because there was no answering smile. Because the badly-painted lips were compressed now, the brown eyes bulged like brandy balls. We know your sort, they said. Thought you'd get away with it, I dare say. The idea!

The girl whose name began with B paid the bill, adding a tip that was taken without thanks, just as though it were a bribe. She looked round desperately. The lights on the other side of the shop were off already, everyone else had gone. She hadn't noticed them, but had they noticed her? Were they at this moment saying to one another, 'Did you notice that odd girl in blue? Wouldn't surprise me to know the police were after her'? She gave a breathless laugh at her own folly, and fairly ran out of the shop. An instant later she heard a key turn in the lock, a blind was drawn down. CLOSED said a forbidding notice and, while she watched from the pavement, the last lights went out.

Now it was quite dark outside, away from the lights. Presently a few couples would come out and drape the benches, or walk, whispering and giggling down the iron steps to the beach, but this was zero hour. People were having high tea in the boarding-houses, getting ready for dinner in the hotels, getting their own meals at home, waiting eagerly for the return of a husband, a daughter, a friend. A flowerseller by the pavement thrust some flowers upon her, but she shook her head. He came after her, pressing his wares.

'Very cheap,' he insisted.

'Don't molest me,' she flared, with such anger that he stood rooted to the spot, shocked, astounded.

'There's a lady,' he shouted after her.

But he was no more shocked than she. What on earth had come over her to speak like that? After all, he had to get a living like everyone else, and didn't the world approve private enterprise? *The plums of life won't drop though long you stop, But by the hand outstretched they may be fetched.* What put *that* doggerel into her head at this precise moment? Perhaps it had hung over her bed in her nursery in the Never-Never Land to which, she was beginning to fear, she might never return. Historians recount strange tales of people who are apparently born adult; they appear, suddenly full-grown, in a community, with no past history, no ties. No one knows whence they come, not apparently even themselves, an army of living ghosts, an army to which she in future might belong.

She passed a glassed-in shelter, beloved of invalids when the wind blew or the rain descended. An elderly woman, wrapped in a light-coloured fur coat and partially covered by a rug, was sitting erect in a bath-chair, her face red with passion, her hat askew. As the girl drew abreast, she called imperiously.

B stopped, surprised.

'Were you speaking to me?'

'I wasn't talking to myself. Where is she?'

'She?'

'What's the matter? Are you a parrot? Have you seen anyone, coming along?'

'No. No one special, that is.'

'She isn't special. Did you see anyone?'

The girl shook her head.

'She should have been here half an hour ago, instead of leaving me to catch my death of cold. Perhaps that's what she wants. That's all anyone wants for you when you're old. Just a trouble, you see. Can't go out gallivanting all the time. No sense of responsibility. Let the State do it, they say. Different when I was young.'

'Can I do anything? Wheel you back anywhere?'

'You?' The hooded eyes gleamed defiance. 'Certainly not. Don't know who you are. Or did *she* send you?'

'I don't know who you're talking about.'

'Gave her a home when her mother died, doesn't have to go out to work, knows she'll get whatever I leave, but never here when she's wanted. Never satisfied. It won't be for long, I tell her, and when I'm lying in the churchyard you may be sorry. Oh yes.' She nodded and the absurd plumes in her hat shook in unison. 'The money's mine,' she said.

The girl's heart sickened, the nightmare came rushing back. 'Perhaps she's had an accident.'

'Then she's no right to have an accident. She should think of me. And of course she hasn't had an accident. Here she comes.'

A tall woman in a heavy brown coat, wearing a grotesque green hat, came hurrying up. Her dark hair was flying, her eyes were fixed and frightened.

'Where have you been?' The words were as savage as a hail of machine-gun bullets.

'I'm sorry, I couldn't help it—really. Perdita got out. I've been hunting everywhere. Oh, I've found her, and it's all right, I'm sure it's all right.'

She grabbed the rail of the bath-chair, swinging it round. Her indignant eyes met the girl's.

'You shouldn't bother strangers,' she said accusingly. 'Can't you see she's not—herself?'

She went off, wheeling the chair with awkward haste. The words stayed behind her, as though they had an existence of their own.

'Not herself,' repeated the girl in a whisper. 'That makes two of us.'

A small exceedingly composed black cat came past on airy feet. 'Are you lost too?' asked B.

She put down her hands to stroke the velvet fur. The green eyes curdled, the claws flashed from their sheath. The cat jumped delicately on to the seat and proceeded to wash her paws. The girl sat down beside her, and at once the cat gave her an affronted glance and fled away. Now the parade was quite empty, no one to be seen; the shadows thickened where the lamps didn't pierce their density.

Fear came up, soft-footed as the cat. Shoo, shoo, she thought, putting out her hands. Keep away. There must be someone somewhere, I can't stay here all night, I don't know where to go, no one takes you at a hotel without luggage, even if you have the money for your bill. If I were a man it would be different, because I could tell some story, but a girl's always suspect. I may not remember who I am, but at least I know that much.

A closer search of the bag revealed nothing overlooked; despairingly she plunged her hand into her coat pocket, felt something soft crumpled into a corner. She drew it out, a pink slip of paper, held it, unfolded, beneath the light that illuminated the shelter, and relief broke over her like a tidal wave. For the bit of paper, thrust so carelessly into her pocket, was a receipt for a packet left at the railway station at Beachampton that very day. Despair turned tail and vanished, hope sprang up like the proverbial giant refreshed. Now, now the mystery would be resolved. The missing insurance card would be in the case, of course; naturally you wouldn't carry it about with you, not when your bag might be snatched or you might be careless and lose it. She went down the steps to the nearest bus stop, and joined a short queue.

'Do I get a bus to the station from here?' she asked someone just in front of her.

A woman with a sallow frog-shaped face twisted her head over her shoulder.

'Central or west?' she demanded gruffly.

'Central or . . . ? Oh, Central,' she plunged.

'You're the wrong side of the road.' The woman was looking at her rather oddly, wasn't she? The girl turned away with a mutter of thanks, and there was a policeman coming down the street. Was it fancy or did he look at her particularly, too? She darted across the road so quickly she almost overset a motor-cyclist speeding home. The cyclist half rose and shouted, his head over his shoulder, 'If you want to commit suicide, what's wrong with asp*irines*?' (What, indeed?) She had a moment of terror in case the policeman came over to ask her name, but at that moment a bus drew up and she jumped on.

'Station?' said the conductress a minute later. 'We don't go to the station. If you don't know, why don't you ask? You want a 14. Get off at the next stop.'

It was a nightmare all right, the kind where every turn in the road reveals a new obstruction, where every wall conceals an enemy and every step may precipitate you into a grave. She got off, waited an interminable time, and at last mounted the No. 14 bus. By now she was convinced the luggage office would be closed.

'But I must have my bag,' she insisted to herself. 'I must have it. It's my last hope. If it is closed, I'll find the station-master, I'll say, I'll say . . .'

She found she was talking to herself so vigorously that the people on either side were staring. Abruptly she fell silent, and at last she reached the station and tumbled out.

After so many pinpricks she couldn't believe it when the man in the cloakroom, after a cursory glance at the ticket, brought her a neat zip-over blue bag and handed it to her without a word. She almost snatched it up, looking round for some place where she could open it, unperceived. There must be a waiting-room, a ladies' room, on every station, and so there was, but they were the other side of the barrier. Her eye

fell on a chalked board of train arrivals, and she saw that one
was expected from London in the course of the next few
minutes. Hurriedly she bought a platform ticket.

'London train, arrival, I mean.'

'Platform two, down the stairs,' said the ticket collector,
indifferently.

She found the waiting-room that held two or three people,
some children, a brown and white dog on a lead. She paid no
attention to any of them and they didn't notice her. She set the
bag on the seat, pulled the zipper (thank goodness, it wasn't
locked), and looked inside. There wasn't much there, just what a
girl would take who was planning to be away for a long week-
end. A nylon nightdress, travelling slippers, washing materials
in a blue and white striped case, a hairbrush in an embroidered
bag, cosmetics, not many but all good quality and all matching,
panties, brassière, stockings, handkerchiefs in a second
embroidered bag, a dress, neatly rolled, a cardigan, a pair of
shoes. Well packed, not as if someone had tossed them in
anyhow in a burning hurry to get away—but no card, no books,
nothing personal at all. The label in the dress showed it came
from a big London store, designed by a famous name and mass
produced; the belt with its plain silver buckle told her nothing.
Anyone could own the underclothes and the cosmetics. There
wasn't a letter or a cheque-book or a scrap of handwriting
anywhere.

The train from London came in and the other people in the
waiting-room boarded it; it was going farther along the coast. A
few people got out and made for the exit. No one came into the
waiting-room. She zipped up the bag again and walked away
from the station. Now it was approaching seven o'clock, she
must make some plan for the night. Instinct turned her away
from the big hotels, no one wants to be bothered with a newcomer who hasn't booked when there's dinner to be dished up.
Besides, if she was on the run. . . . On the run! What on earth
put that idea into her head? You didn't have to be on the run
not to go to the police—that's where inquiries would be made.
She hesitated in front of the smaller establishments, private
hotels they were called, passed two and rang the bell of the

third. The proprietress scarcely gave her a glance. Sorry, full up, she declared. The next hotel said the same, and the next. She had made a mistake asking for a room for the night; at this hour it wasn't worth the trouble, too little profit when you remembered the cost of laundry, and staff didn't like being asked to make up beds at this hour. If she'd said a week the answer would have been different.

She abandoned the hotels and tried the narrow houses with Bed and Breakfast or Room to Let on cardboard placards in the transoms. The first woman said, 'How long?' staring at the economical luggage.

She had gleaned a little sense by this time. 'About a week, I think. I'm waiting for a letter from London.'

'Ah! I don't do nothing but breakfast.'

'That's all right. I can get my other meals out. Do you mean you have a room?'

'I couldn't rightly say. Is that all your luggage?'

She improvised hurriedly. 'The rest's at the docks. This is just till I go on board.'

'The docks? And staying here a week?' You could see open disbelief in the woman's eye.

'The lease of my flat in London is up,' explained the distracted girl, 'so I thought I'd have a few days at the sea before I sailed.'

Never explain, never apologise—someone said that, someone who knew his onions.

'I see.' The voice grudged her even an attic. 'Well, come up.'

The room was small, under the roof, with sloping walls and a tunnel to the window. The bed had been bought second-hand at a sale of prison effects, from the feel of it. There was a broken-down gas fire, a chair, a table and a spotted glass.

'Two shillings extra for the electric,' said the woman sharply. 'It's not often I have a room to let.'

'How much?' It was a horrid room in a horrid house, with a horrid woman in charge, but at least it had four walls and you could shut the door and be alone.

'Three guineas, seeing it's out of the season.'

It was too much, she knew it was too much. 'A week?'

'Well, not a day. Though, mind you, in the season, I've had fifteen shillings a night and no service. Breakfast half a crown plain, four shillings full. That means bacon *and* egg. I was never one to stint my lodgers.'

B looked round desperately. You couldn't stay here a week....

'Pay in advance,' said the grim voice. 'Mind you, I did promise a lady first refusal till seven, but it's nigh that now, and she hasn't come back, and I can't be expected to wait, can I?'

The girl grasped at the providential straw. 'Oh, but if she said she was coming, she may be counting on it, and not find it easy to get in anywhere else at this hour. I don't think I should take advantage...'

She had snatched up the bag and was pressing on to the landing, down the stairs, out of this house of doom, even if it only meant sitting up in the station all night, assuming they'd let you.

'Where's the 'urry?' demanded the woman, following fast. She had a sallow bun of a face, with eyes like the two solitary currants the economical baker had allowed. 'I didn't say she *was* coming, I only said...'

The girl pulled the door open. 'Someone's coming now, I expect that's her.'

She was out of the house and down the street, not even feeling the weight of the bag, in her haste to be gone. The landlady halted in the hall: she knew it was too late. The other woman in the street wasn't coming here, because she didn't exist. They never do.

'In some sort of trouble, you could see that with half an eye,' she consoled herself going back to the kitchen and wondering a bit miserably about the four empty rooms there was no prospect of filling now before Easter. 'Well, I don't want *that* kind in my house.'

Half an hour later the luck had turned. The girl was settled in a comfortable, pleasant room in another Bed and Breakfast house, bathroom adjoining, two guineas a week including breakfast, three baths a week without charge.

'Just come on the London train?' suggested Mrs Lee. 'How about dinner? Are you going out for that or would you like something on a tray?'

'Would that be a lot of trouble?'

Wonderful not to have to brave surprised stares, share a table, most likely, with someone who might try to get into conversation.

'Could you really?'

'I don't do dinners as a rule,' explained the landlady, 'but seeing it's out of the season. . . . '

The tray came up at eight o'clock, a nice bit of fish with boiled potatoes and tinned peas, tinned fruit and custard, a cup of tea. Three and six and cheap at the price.

'Got a hot-water-bottle, dear? You might want one. It's turned chilly. Let's see, four nights, was it?'

'I—I'm not quite sure. I have to telephone to-morrow.'

'We don't have the phone.'

(Thank goodness for that.) 'I'll go along to the post office. As a matter of fact, there might be a letter. I couldn't leave an address.'

Don't pile it on, common sense warned her. *Words divide and rend but Silence is most noble to the end.* Safer, too.

After the tray had gone down again, the endless evening stretched ahead of her like walking down a road and thinking every turn must bring you to a bus stop or a lighted garage, and every time there's nothing but darkness ahead. She wished there was a wireless in the room, anything to distract her from her thoughts, which were simply an arrow pointing nowhere. She had a fresh shock when Mrs Lee brought up the Visitors' Book.

'They're ever so strict down here. I've brought a pen,' she said.

She knew an instant of real panic. What was she to write? B—that was easy. Barbara, the first name that came into her mind. But Barbara what? Her eyes turned towards the wall. There was a water-colour of cows in a field. Barbara Field. London. She wrote it down hastily. The landlady looked at the scrawled signature.

'Miss Field?'

'Of course.'

Mrs Lee nodded and went away. What was she thinking of? That I've left a husband and am using my unmarried name? Well, that's no crime, in fact, it would be as good a story as any, if I needed a story, but of course I don't, because by this time to-morrow everything will be cleared up. It's like a cloud over the sun, that's all, or a mild attack of eye-trouble. A film floats over the eyeball and for the moment you don't see a thing, but presently it floats off again. And mine will float away.

Will it? Why?

Because it must, of course, that's why. Because anything else would be unthinkable. Because it would mean I was mad.

A fresh thought struck her. Suppose, as was most likely, when she woke to-morrow she was back in her real self. Would she remember to-day? Didn't you sometimes hear of people who had lost a day out of their lives and never recovered it, didn't know where they'd been, what they'd done, it could be any-thing—murder, arson—a split personality, they said, there was a name for it, but she couldn't remember it. She hadn't done anything, of course, except sit on the front—no harm in that—unless, before she woke up on the bench—unless there was something that had brought her down to Beachampton in the first place, something she couldn't endure to remember, so Nature had thrown up a barrier.

Don't let thought go that way. That way real madness lies.

It seemed quite a good idea, though, to note down every-thing she remembered of the past three hours, so that when she woke in a strange room to-morrow she'd know how she got there. She looked round, glad of the opportunity for distraction, but there was no paper to be seen, not so much as a used envelope. Nor was there a label tied on the bag, as she'd hoped, because that, at least, would have given her her name. She hesitated about interrupting Mrs Lee, but it was the lesser of two evils, so she went timidly as far as the hall and called.

'So stupid of me,' she gabbled when the woman opened the

door at the far end. 'I've forgotten to pack any writing-paper. I wonder—perhaps I should send a line—giving an address, I mean. . . .'

'I'll bring it up in a minute, dear,' said Mrs Lee firmly.

'I don't want to trouble you.' The perspiration of fear had begun to break out all over her.

'That's all right. I won't be more than a minute.'

What do you want that minute for? she wondered desperately, turning back to the stairs. Ring up the police? But no, she couldn't do that, because there wasn't a phone. Got someone down there, perhaps. . . .

Mrs Lee came up a minute later, carrying a cheap yellowish writing-pad and some envelopes that didn't quite match. She looked very grave.

'Miss Field, there's something I should have asked you,' she said. 'Are you over twenty-one?'

'Yes. Oh yes. Of course I am. I'm twenty-three, actually.'

(Was there a law that forbade you to stay in an apartment house if you were under age?)

'Oh? You look younger. Now you just listen to me. I can see you're in some sort of trouble, and I don't want to seem interfering, but—why don't you ring up your Mum and tell her where you are? I know how it is, I've had daughters of my own, something happens, you fly off the handle and out you go. But it's always a mistake. Really it is. As I said, I haven't got the telephone here, but my neighbour next door would let you use hers, and she's not the nosy kind that would listen, I can promise you that.'

The temptation to confide in this kind woman was almost overwhelming, but she beat it down. Because she'd say at once, 'Lost your memory? That's bad. Been ill perhaps. Now you just put on your hat and I'll come with you and we'll go round to the police. Someone may have put out a message for you. Now, there's nothing to be afraid of, if you haven't done anything wrong.'

If—if! But had she? How could she tell? And how explain this instinctive, horrified shrinking from the thought of them, unless she was in serious trouble? No, no, wait till to-morrow when you'd remember who you were and could make plans then. Don't be stampeded.

She looked up to find the woman watching her gravely.

'My mother's dead,' she gulped. Odd, how sure she was that that was true, when she wasn't sure about anything else—except that she didn't want to go near the station.

'Then—you weren't living alone in London, were you?'

Perhaps she'd always been the imaginative type, how could she tell? Perhaps she was an author and had had a brainstorm, the sort of thing you could easily suppose might happen to people who wrote books, spending all their time with undisguised unreality, as she'd once heard it described. And there was a story she'd read once, though where and in what circumstances she couldn't tell you, about a man who brooded so long over a picture of a boat on a lake that eventually he brooded himself into the boat, inside the picture, and when the landlady came up to his room he'd gone, and no one ever saw him in the flesh again. No, think of something else. And like a flash the reasonable, the quite probable answer was supplied.

'I used to live with my father,' she explained.

Mrs Lee met her more than half-way. 'You mean he's married again and you don't get on with your stepma?'

'A girl of my own age,' improvised Barbara, swiftly.

'I see. Well. Don't do anything silly. Things generally settle down, you know, and one of these days you'll be having your own home, a pretty girl like you.'

She smiled kindly and went away. Barbara stared down at her ringless hand, then she lifted it nearer to the light. It was true there was no ring on it now, but—was it fancy or was there the faintest of indentations, as though for some time there had been a ring there? Am I escaping from a husband? Did he threaten me? Did I threaten him? Is there some good reason behind my feeling where the police are concerned? I don't know, I don't know. That was what it all came back to, those three words—I don't know.

She took up the writing-pad and wrote steadily for a short time, recording all she could remember of the day, which admittedly wasn't much, but might fill a gap when she woke in the morning. Perhaps she had lost herself in sleep, taken a wrong turning and, in sleep, would retrace her steps and find herself at home once more.

CHAPTER 2

She opened her eyes to the unfamiliar room and the sound of church bells. With a shock she realised it must be Sunday, and she hadn't gone back through the wall as she had hoped, was still Barbara Field with no past and a problematical future. After breakfast she went out and bought the Sunday papers, in case there was a hue and cry for a girl who'd disappeared yesterday from—where?—last seen wearing a blue coat, etc., and perhaps a smudged photograph even a mother wouldn't recognise. But there was nothing, not even in the paper that specialises in heart-throbs. Some missing women there were, true, but none of them could conceivably be herself. For one thing, they'd been missing too long. True, she didn't know when she disappeared out of her own world, but she had only parked the case yesterday and it seemed improbable that she had been wandering about before then. And whoever she was no one had missed her to the extent of putting out a public call. Once again she considered approaching the police, once again she shied from the idea. Wait a little, she thought, I may come back to myself as suddenly as I was lost. Anyway, nothing could happen on a Sunday—that was illogical, she knew, but she didn't stop to wonder why—and by Monday it might be all right. That she might find herself in a worse fix when she did get back she didn't pause to consider.

She didn't know if she usually went to church, but she was afraid of Mrs Lee coming up with further questions and proposals, and once Mrs Lee got the idea there was something really wrong, not just a family disagreement, she'd be round to the sign of the blue light in two shakes of a drake's tail.

Besides, at church something familiar might set old chords throbbing, and you couldn't afford to disregard any chance when you were in her shoes. But it didn't, though she seemed at home in the service, standing and kneeling at all the appropriate times, so she couldn't be an absolute stranger to public worship, and at least she didn't attract any attention here as she had done on the parade last night. She took her lunch at a restaurant on the sea-front, and then sat in a shelter, reading the papers line by line, in case anything, a name-place, say, aroused an echo. London, Nottingham, Coventry, Newcastle-on-Tyne—they were no more than words. She read through all the human stories because there might be a surname that would help, but that was no good either. Afterwards, because it was a fine blowy afternoon, and she couldn't spend it at Mrs Lee's, she rode on a bus over the downs and had tea at a little place with a pair of blue budgerigars twittering in a cage in the window, and when she got back she had high tea at another café and went to church again, to kill time really. And after that it was time to go back to the apartment house. Before she went to sleep that night she had reached one conclusion. She couldn't go on killing time, while she waited for things to right themselves; she must look for a job of some sort while she waited for the miracle.

'I wonder what sort of job I did before,' she debated. She took it for granted she had been working, everyone worked these days. Her hands were well kept, pretty, faintly-coloured, with well kept nails, hands that had had care lavished on them. But only the palest of nail varnish and the nails themselves were neatly cut. She decided she must have left her job very recently—did *that* have anything to do with her loss of memory?—because of the notes in her bag. Surely she didn't generally carry twelve pounds around with her? And then she had lost herself on a Saturday, the end of a week, everything fitted. Was I sacked? she thought. If so, why? For dishonesty? Oh no. She shuddered away from the thought; but it would fit in with her instinctive dread of the police. Well then, what had she been? A secretary (but she didn't know shorthand, she was sure of that)—a model, a nurse, a film extra? Nothing seemed

21

to stand out from the rest. People were always remarking what a small world it was, so one day, quite soon perhaps, she would run up against someone she used to know.

'Why, Bertha—or Brunhilde—or perhaps even Barbara,' they would say, 'fancy meeting you here.'

And instantly the wheels would start revolving and the cloud would shift, and everything would be all right. In the meantime, it was work or the police, and that really meant no choice at all.

The long day was over at last, and this time she went to bed without much hope that next morning she would see a face she recognised when she looked in the glass. And she was right. Nothing had changed. Nor was there anything in this morning's papers to solve her perplexity; but the bright sun and the dancing sea were encouraging, and she went out to the Public Library where the authorities pasted up a list of Situations Vacant. Because, naturally, she couldn't go to an employment bureau. They would demand references, and she'd be expected to produce her insurance card. The absence of that was a fearful blow. You couldn't hope for work without a card, and though you might get through the first week by saying you'd lost it and were waiting for a duplicate, that wouldn't take you far. She seemed to remember that if you worked for one employer for less than eight hours a week you didn't need to have your card stamped, and presumably there were always people wanting a cleaner or help with children. But it wasn't much of a prospect.

In any case there was nothing in to-day's list that she felt competent to apply for; she moved away and studied the handwritten advertisements in the window of a stationer's shop; various people wanted cleaners, references essential, or temporary chamber-maids, or had a play-pen or a second-hand piano or some old clothes to sell. Inquire inside for address, they said, concealing themselves under a box number. She found a lot of shops with these little cases full of advertisements, and bought a notebook and put down some of the addresses, but though in the course of the next two or three days she applied for any that seemed suitable—slave jobs for the most part—she met with no success. Either no one answered her written application or they seemed to decide on sight she wouldn't do for them. It was on the Thursday morning, when her money was running low and hope was sinking likewise, that she saw the advertisement. It was in the local paper, brought up with the breakfast tray by good-natured Mrs Lee—*You may as well have a read of this, dear, I shan't have a minute till teatime.* It ran:

Good pay and easy conditions offered to a young lady, aged 21–23, who is not afraid of unconventional duties. She should be well-educated, imaginative, sympathetic and without family ties. This is a temporary post, but treatment will be generous to the right person, who should be able to respect confidences. Only those with the stated qualifications and within the stated age limit, who are free to undertake work immediately, can be considered.

And there followed an initial and a box number.

Barbara read this astonishing advertisement twice. On the face of it, it appeared an invitation to disaster.

('And they say men are the adventurous sex,' that unconventional London lawyer, Arthur Crook, was to remark not so many weeks later. 'What on earth did you think it was, sugar?'

And she answered gently, 'I thought it was an answer to prayer.')

She penned a neat application and ran down to the post; after she had shot the envelope through the slit of the letterbox, not giving herself time to change her mind, she walked along the front, planning the story she would tell if an interview were vouchsafed her. She would have to be a lot more careful with details now than when she had allowed romantically-minded Mrs Lee to half-fashion her story for her; but she needn't be too finicky, because it was obvious there was something screwy, as Crook would say, about the whole set-up. And of course you had to remember that, whatever happened, hers was a unique position. What can the law do to somebody who virtually doesn't exist?

Mrs Lee brought up the reply twenty-four hours later.

'Perhaps this is the letter you've been expecting,' she beamed, not snoopily, but in the voice of a kind neighbour.

'I believe it may be,' Barbara agreed, looking at the clear adult handwriting. No suggestion of lunacy there, at least, but of course it might just be crime. The one thing she was convinced of was that it wouldn't be a straight-forward run-of-the-line job.

The postmark was Preston-on-Sea which she knew was a rather stylish suburb of Beachampton, and the address on the letter was The Hall. But the rendezvous was to take place at the Beaulieu Hotel—'in case I don't fit in with the criminal set-up' she told herself dryly. 'Well, the respectable haven't any use for me, so perhaps the crooks will have.'

'You will no doubt have realised that there are peculiar factors about the situation,' observed the writer of the letter, who signed himself Miles Calmady.

Barbara murmured the equivalent of 'And how!'

Mr Calmady wanted her to meet him at 11.30 in the lounge of the hotel. She could reach Preston by bus, and he thoughtfully told her its number and the time that it ran. He seemed as anxious to get hold of her as she to find employment.

It was another bright day and the streets were full of people doing their week-end shopping. She had repeated her story to herself so often that she was beginning to believe it, just as she was beginning to think of herself as Barbara Field. She arrived at the hotel a few minutes before time, and walked into the lounge. Before she could reach the reception desk a tall man in the early thirties got up from a basket-work chair and came towards her. He seemed to have no doubt of her identity, and when she had looked round and seen the average age of the lounge's other occupants she wasn't surprised.

'Miss Field? You're admirably punctual. Come and sit down and we'll have some coffee. While we're waiting for that I'll outline the situation. You're not given to sudden faints or anything, I hope? Good. Tell me, have you travelled much in your time? I see you can't have got far because you haven't had much time.' His charming smile flashed out. 'But have you, for instance, ever been in America?'

She shook her head. It occurred to her that not only was her insurance card missing but also her passport, always supposing she possessed one. Someone—herself?—had taken good care to separate her utterly from her old life.

'No? That's a pity, but it's not insuperable. You look very intelligent, if I may say so; you might even, at a pinch, be able to give the impression you had been there?'

'Is that important?'

'It's the crux of the job. Ah, here comes the coffee. I did warn you it was—unusual. The first thing I must impress on you is the need for absolute secrecy. I'm going to show you my hand—I have no choice there—but if you don't want to play I must ask for your word never to speak of what I've told you to anyone else. By the way, are you living alone?'

'Meaning the family ties? I haven't any. I was working in London, but I wanted a change, so I came down here and then I thought I'd look for work, temporarily at all events, in the neighbourhood.'

'But you're in touch with your family?'

She repeated the story about her father and his mythical second marriage.

'You mean, you haven't written since you got here?'

'I can't write. I haven't any address.'

'On their honeymoon? But they'll come back.'

'I suppose so.' She was purposely indifferent. 'I shall never be going back there, and they won't want me. What will it be to them where I work or what I do? If you're afraid of my spilling the beans in that direction, you can put the idea out of your head. I can promise you they'll never hear a word from me.'

'I say,' he said, 'you're taking this a bit hard, aren't you? No concern of mine, of course. Was the bride a friend of yours?'

'A contemporary.'

'And she's ousted you? You couldn't stand the thought of sitting at the side of the table instead of the head. Have you a proud nature, Barbara Field?'

'I never thought about it till now.'

He laughed. 'You're delicious. What job did you do before you left London? Or didn't you? I suppose you never studied for the stage?'

Considering what a good act she was putting on it seemed just barely possible that she had, but it was best to shake her head.

'Seeing your father's just married again, I suppose there's no likelihood of your having had much to do with sick people?' Miles Calmady went on.

'The advertisement didn't say anything about nursing.'

'Nor have I,' he assured her coolly. 'Anyway, Julie does all the nursing that's necessary. Julie is Mrs Calmady's daughter, and my cousin. You, if you undertake the job, will be Mrs Calmady's granddaughter from America. Now you see why I wondered if you'd done any acting.'

Barbara leaned back in her chair. 'Where's the real granddaughter?' she asked as evenly as she could.

'We've every reason to fear she was lost on the plane that was missing over the Atlantic a week ago. We waited till now in case there was any news. I mean, she might have changed her mind, she sounded a mercurial creature. But there's been no cable, nothing, so we're practically compelled to believe she's gone.'

'And Mrs Calmady doesn't know?'

'And mustn't. In her state of health, she couldn't stand the shock. She's pretty old and very fragile. This girl's mother was her younger daughter, and the apple of her eye. Alice she was christened, but she was always known as Birdie, don't ask me why. Mrs Calmady adored her; nobody was good enough for darling Birdie, though a lot of chaps tried to persuade her they were. Then out of the blue, off Birdie winged with a fellow called Fitton. That'll be your name, by the way—Barbara Fitton.'

'Barbara!' she exclaimed.

'Exactly. That's one of the reasons I picked your letter out of the pile—there was a surprising entry, you may be interested to know. If that's your own name then you'll be attentive for the sound of it, whereas if you'd been christened Lavender, for instance—don't laugh, I once knew a girl who was—you might be day-dreaming and not realise you were being addressed. We can't take any chance of the plan going wrong, and though Mrs Calmady is old and frail she's got nothing wrong with her brain. She must never suspect. You do appreciate that?'

Barbara said simply, 'You must be mad. How could you hope to put over such an impersonation? It's not even as if I'd ever seen the real Barbara Fitton.'

'That matters less than you think, since no one else has ever seen her either. I'll put you in the picture. When Birdie ran off, and that was about as cruel a thing as you can conceive, she went to Canada where Barbara was born. About three years later the marriage went to pieces, I don't know the details, Birdie was as airy as a summer breeze. Joe and I have decided to call it a day, she wrote. She kept the child.'

'There was a divorce?'

'Oh yes, there was a divorce. Her mother begged her to come back and bring the little girl with her, but Birdie wouldn't hear of it. Whether she had some other man up her sleeve or if it was just that she preferred the life out there, I don't know. Anyway, she wouldn't come. But she did agree to send the child back on a visit. Then, before anything definite could be fixed, the war broke out, and it would obviously have been madness to send a child home to Britain. In 1944 Birdie was killed in a road accident, and Mrs Calmady started hoping again. We did hope then, if you remember—but no, of course you won't, you were too young—the war would be over that year. And, while the armies havered, up popped Fitton with a new wife to claim his daughter. Naturally the courts raised no objection. The second Mrs Fitton seems to have been a kind woman who gave the child a home, probably the first real home she'd had since infancy. Birdie had many charms but no more notion of creating a home than a cuckoo. When the war was over Barbara had settled, and Fitton didn't want to let her go. She was about 12 years old and happy in her school, but he wrote quite a kindly letter and said she should come back when she was a bit older. Well, one thing and another, the visit never came off. Then Fitton died and his wife went back to her people.'

'That was Barbara's chance,' suggested the girl.

'Yes. But she didn't take it. Every year there was some reason why she couldn't make the trip this summer. First she wanted to graduate, then she was engaged and she and her husband would come to England on their honeymoon, then the engagement was broken off. The long and the short of it is that no definite plan was made until this spring. She announced her intention of flying over, and—well, the rest you know.'

'There's one point that occurs to me,' said Barbara. 'If she had been on board, wouldn't you have had an official notification?'

'Not necessarily, though of course we had considered that. There's no special reason why she should have given us as next-of-kin, and then it wasn't one of the regular lines, and there may not have been any regulation to that effect. But I cabled and was told that she did, in fact, take her passage and there's no record of her not turning up, so it seems probable she was on board and did lose her life.'

'It would be awkward if she suddenly appeared and found me wearing her shoes,' Barbara suggested.

'I'd strangle her if she tried to make trouble for Mrs Calmady,' he said, with a ferocity that startled her. 'But I don't think that point will arise. Now, how do you feel about it? Now I've met you and talked to you for a little I believe you'd fill the bill admirably.'

'It's not a thing to be settled in five minutes. Do you know what Barbara Fitton looked like? She might have been small and dark.'

'Not from the information we have. There's a letter from Birdie—fortunately her mother kept every line she wrote, treasured it as if it were gold leaf, though it wouldn't amount to much of a fortune at that—saying that anyone would know the child was hers. Birdie, according to Julie who naturally remembers her better than I do, was about your height, very fair, an English complexion. You're approximately the right age, there are no photographs except one or two snapshots that could easily be you or almost any girl of similar build, there are two or three letters from her that you can get by heart before you see the old lady—Julie has managed to abstract them—but it'll be safe to draw on your imagination most of the time. It's not such a risk as you seem to think,' he went on quickly. 'Mrs Calmady's very weak, you won't have to do a lot of talking, and if she refers to things in your mother's youth you've only to say you don't remember or you don't think she ever spoke of it. You were only ten when she died.'

'What sort of a temperament have I got?' she demanded. 'Am I callous or adventurous or timid?'

'Well, not the last, not if you're Birdie's daughter. I've often wondered if the old lady really saw through her, she's pretty shrewd, but kept up a front, really for self-defence because she couldn't bear to accept the truth, which was that Birdie had about as much heart as a china dog. Why, after her marriage broke up she wrote—I've seen the letter—saying she knew it wouldn't last for ever, but it had been good fun and to-morrow is also a day.'

'That might have been her form of self-defence,' the girl argued. 'A form of courage.'

'Or a form of callousness. It was pretty callous the way she walked out on the old lady, apparently without a qualm.'

'It was a matter of conflicting loyalties,' insisted Barbara. 'When you're in love, and nothing short of love would explain her action, nothing and nobody else counts at all. In a way, you could say they didn't exist.'

She stopped dead, an amazed look on her face. How do I know that? she wondered. The only answer was that she'd worn Birdie's shoes at some time, which would explain the mark on her finger where surely a ring had once rested.

Miles Calmady regarded her with interest. 'That's good,' he said, 'that's very good indeed. You might play that card when you see the old lady. She'd appreciate it. She really did love her daughter more than her own life, and she'd admire you, love you even, for trying to stand up for your mother. I don't see why it shouldn't all work out very well,' he added, thoughtfully, pinching his lower lip between his thumb and forefinger. 'You look right—I wonder if she'll notice you haven't a Canadian accent? No, don't try and adopt one, because it 'ud be sure to sound phony. And you grew up with your mother for several years, so it probably will seem natural to her that you should have an English timbre to your voice. Anyway, that's a chance we shall have to take.'

'I don't like it,' said Barbara flatly. 'Deceiving an old woman on her death-bed. Supposing I can't pull it off, that would be worse than knowing the truth.'

Face and voice changed at once. 'My dear Miss Field, you are not being employed not to pull it off. You have the necessary qualifications, if you choose to use them. If you have conscientious scruples, make sure they're not rooted in self-interest. What, after all, are you being asked to do? Bring some peace and reassurance to an old lady whose life hasn't been by any means a piece of cake. Is that such an immoral thing to do? Suppose I'd said we simply wanted you to act as her companion? You wouldn't have jibbed at that. Well, in a sense that's what we are asking, only you have to assume a blood tie, which shouldn't put too great a strain on your capacities. What's the matter?'

For Barbara was strangling a most inappropriate gust of laughter. Too great a strain on her capacities, indeed, when already she was assuming a personality that didn't exist! Barbara Fitton, Barbara Field, what did it matter what she called herself?

'You make it sound like—like a piece of cake,' she told him. 'How long would this go on?'

'Not long. Her heart's in a shocking state. You might say it's only the hope, the expectation, of seeing her beloved Birdie's daughter, that has kept it beating at all. We've had a bad time this week, when the girl didn't arrive. We had to stall her, say there was a setback and the plane had to return to base, and Barbara was waiting for another passage. You might remember that, by the way.'

'Who else will know about it? Have I got to deceive the whole household?'

'We're not Buckingham Palace,' he pointed out. 'The household consists of Mrs Calmady and her daughter, Julie—unmarried, madly jealous of Birdie (you must keep that in mind)—and myself. I'm not there most of the time, I'm manager of a local engineering business, but I live at the house for the time being, mainly at Mrs Calmady's request. I haven't a wife, so there won't be any contemporary females to get in your hair. Julie, of course, will know the truth, and we've had to confide in Dr Stuart. He agreed it would be fatal to tell Mrs Calmady the truth. There's a woman who comes in by the day, and to her you will be Barbara Fitton. I think she's more or less half-witted, so I don't think she constitutes much of a danger. But there are a few things to bear in mind. For instance, do you have your name in any of your clothes?'

'No.' If only she had it would have solved her problem days ago.

'Initials on your handkerchiefs, say?'

'Only B.'

'Then—personal papers. Keep your handbag with you, wherever you are. And—don't give your address away to anyone. It will be obvious to you that we can't risk letters coming addressed to Miss Field. Would this landlady where you're staying let you use her address? Then you could go over and collect them.'

'I'm sure she would. Not that there'll be many.'

'We don't want to leave any earths unstopped. As for Mrs Calmady herself, I don't think you need trouble over her. People on the whole see what they expect to see. She'll be expecting Birdie's daughter, and it won't occur to her you could be anyone else.'

He talked her round. In her heart she grasped at this somewhat dubious straw. At all events, she would have a roof over her head and time, that most precious of all commodities, and perhaps in a new circle something would happen to break the spell and by the time she was free to leave she would be herself again. Like a dormouse going round on its wheel, she always returned to that point.

They discussed terms. 'A lump sum of fifty pounds,' he said, and her keep while she was with them. Anything the old lady might give her as Barbara Fitton would naturally not hold good.

'You're taking a big chance,' said Barbara, perceiving this aspect for the first time, 'I might be an adventuress, out for what I could get. And it would be awkward for you, explaining the truth.'

'Sauce for the goose,' he told her. 'You'd have to prove your identity, and if we all stand solid and swear we thought you were the real Miss Fitton. . . . But come, we're wasting time. We're neither of us going to do any double-crossing; and if a miracle happens and the old lady takes on a new lease of life, well, you won't find us ungenerous, I can promise you. In a way, I believe it may be lucky for her that her precious granddaughter can't come in person. She gave me the impression of being very hard-boiled, and you've got to make up a lot of leeway.'

'I'll do my best,' she promised, suddenly carried away by the pathos of the situation. 'When do I start?'

'Go back and collect your things and I'll pick you up at Beachampton Station. You'll have come from the Airport, remember. We don't have to fuss too much about the precise time the plane touched down, because that won't pass through the old lady's mind. You were flying all night, of course—just go over the obvious details in your mind. And take heart.' He took her hand in his in a warm and friendly grasp. 'It'll be all right. I'm convinced of it. Appearances may be very deceptive, but nothing would make me believe you weren't on the level.'

If only you knew, she thought, as she hurried back to the bus stop. If only you knew. She might have been interested to see into Miles Calmady's mind. Nice girl, he was thinking, in some sort of a jam. Cagey. Could be she's bolting from someone—I don't think it's the father, she was almost too confiding there. But if she wants to lie low, that's all to the good, because it won't bother her if the job goes on a little longer than we anticipate.

He drove his car into the gates of The Hall to tell his cousin, Julie, to kill the fatted calf and prepare the old lady for the long-awaited news.

CHAPTER 3

Julie Calmady stood at the window, half-concealed by the curtain, awaiting the arrival of the pseudo-Barbara Fitton. Miles had gone to meet her, and the old lady, Julie's mother, was bubbling over with anticipation.

'Now, Mother, do keep calm or you'll have a stroke before she arrives,' Julie had said.

She was a woman of forty-eight, thin and dark, with a sallow skin and rather small eyes set on either side a long questing nose; she could never have been attractive, and she had reached middle age without developing that quality of humorous acceptance of her own limitations that makes the lives of many elderly single women tolerable. She had fiercely opposed her cousin's suggestion when it was first made.

'It's wicked,' she had declared, 'imposing on an old woman, who's feeble and half-blind.'

'That's just why we can afford to take the risk,' he insisted. 'She won't see the girl, only her granddaughter, and that's the last thing she wants to see this side the grave.'

'It's not fair,' muttered Julie, but she wasn't now thinking of her mother and the strange girl. 'Life's never been fair,' she thought. 'Why should it always have been Birdie who had Mother's love? Birdie the men ran after, Birdie who could get away with lies and cheating? I was always honest, I believed in doing your duty. Why, I've given Mother my whole life, but now she's dying she'd sooner see Miles than me, and a hundred times sooner see Birdie's daughter.'

And now that she was dying, you could be sure it would be with Birdie's name on her lips, that her last cry would be for the girl who'd never even heard of her before this morning. I don't know what I'd do without Julie, she'd say, but it didn't mean anything. And of course she could have done without her. All she wanted now was someone to look after her, and—face it—a stranger would be less clumsy, less apprehensive in a sick-room, and someone new to listen to her maunderings about her darling Birdie.

'Why, I've never had any life of my own,' Julie discovered. 'And when she goes I shall have nothing, because I gave it away years ago and it's too late now to claim it back.'

The sound of a car stopping at the door brought her thoughts back to the present situation. Miles was standing on the pavement, helping a girl to get out. Julie, who had long sight, thought with a pang, 'Why, she might almost be Birdie's daughter, tall and fair and quite, quite beautiful.' There was no sense denying that. This stranger, this interloper, turned and looked up at the house, and there was something about the face, young and gentle and touched with a sort of hope, that made Julie's tired heart contract. Anyone would believe a girl who looked like that. Only anyone might be wrong. *Don't leave your handbag unattended.* Mr Merion had put in the church porch. *Pious-looking old ladies are often the worst thieves.* And who's to say that gentle girls with candid expressions aren't the biggest cheats on record? No girl who hadn't got something to hide would have accepted the commission in the first place. And yet hers was the only letter Miles had seriously considered. And no wonder! All the rest, and there had been a surprising number of applications, had proclaimed themselves even on paper for what they were, girls who hoped they were on to a good thing, and who weren't scrupulous, who let it be known they were what they'd call sports. And even Julie had to admit there'd been something about this girl's letter that rang true, which only went to show, of course, that she was cleverer than the others, more experienced, realised that a big house, with a rich old woman at the helm, was money for jam as she'd put it. Poor Julie! She was too muddled to remember that the advertisement hadn't given anything away.

She supposed they'd cooked up some story that would hold

water, she only hoped they'd have the decency to let her know what it was, step by precarious step.

The door-bell rang and Florrie went to answer it. She supposed Miles wanted to introduce her right away. They weren't confiding in Florrie, of course, even Miles realised the absurdity of that. She was a good worker, if her brain wasn't her strong point, but her tongue was like the dormouse's tail, that went on and on. She'd never keep her mouth shut, and really you couldn't blame her, with a lovely jammy story like this to tell. She wasn't a local woman, not in their sense of the word, had come down from London with her children during the war, and stayed after the children grew up. A reliable woman in the sense that she wouldn't read your letters, probably couldn't read, come to that, thought Julie maliciously, with no ideas in her head beyond the pictures and a cup of tea, an unfortunate wife, in the sense that she'd been deserted, and thinking it as good as a film, the young lady turning up when they'd practically given up hope. Julie knew that in Florrie Kemp's mind at this instant there was a vision of a lovely, golden-haired girl kneeling by her grandmother's bed.

'*And you came all across the world for my sake, my darling?*'

'*All across the world, Grandmother.*'

Julie gave herself a shake and went down to greet the newcomer.

As she'd anticipated, Florrie was standing in the hall, gaping.

'Is this all the luggage?' she demanded, grabbing the blue zip bag.

'The rest's coming by sea,' said the stranger calmly. (Oh, she was a cool one!) 'Of course I had another case but there was an accident, you heard that, and I thought I could buy whatever else I needed on this side.'

'It doesn't matter about anything else,' said Miles quickly. 'You brought yourself, that's the main thing. This is your Aunt Julie,' he went on in cool tones.

Julie gasped with rage. Of course, it was all for Florrie's benefit, she realised that, but now she was face to face with the situation she wasn't sure she'd be able to cope with it.

'Is your mother ready to see Barbara now?' Miles went on.

'Ready? She's panting. If I've told her once about the accident and the cable I've told her twenty times. Barbara had better get herself tidied up and I'll prepare Mother.'

'Mightn't it be better for me to go straight to her room?' suggested the girl. 'She won't notice if I'm not looking like a bandbox.'

'Sweet!' breathed Florrie. Felicity Fane in *Twice Nought is Nothing* had said something very like that at the local Odeon last week.

'I'll take her up,' said Julie, in a voice that brooked no argument. At the turn of the stairs she caught the girl fiercely by the elbow.

'Be careful,' she warned her, 'everything depends on you. Mind you, I never approved of the idea. . . .'

'I hope before the end you will,' the girl whispered back. 'I promise I'll do my best.'

There was something hurried and sweet about her young voice, the earnestness of her look, the sincerity, you'd say, if you didn't know she was play-acting.

'I suppose that's your job,' remarked Julie in ruthless tones, refusing to be softened and pausing on the next floor.

'My job?'

'Acting, I mean. Well, if we had to get someone for a charade I suppose an actress was our best bet. And don't forget, whatever your record on the stage, you have a leading rôle here.'

She opened a door and said in her gruff, ungracious way, 'Here's Barbara, Mother. She's just arrived. Now remember,' she added in a hectoring tone turning back to the girl, 'your grandmother isn't strong. . . .'

On the pillow an old head turned. Old eyes that had been as blue as a lake regained some of their colour through the tears of weakness and joy that suffused them.

'I can't believe it.' The words were no more than a breath between the colourless lips. 'My darling, is it really you?'

Barbara knew a sudden access of confidence. There was no need to act here, you just had to follow your own eager heart.

She was across the room, bending over the bed with the old veined hands held fast in hers, that were warm and reassuring.

'I'm here,' she said, 'and I'll stay as long as you want me. I'm only sorry I didn't get here before.'

'It doesn't matter. It doesn't matter at all, now that you are here at last. Oh, I've longed so much to see Birdie's daughter before I die.'

'Don't talk of dying in my first five minutes. It's been such a long time.'

'I thought you'd never come. Don't let go of my hands, they seem to hold me to life. Julie, set the lamp where I can see her better. Are you like your mother, my darling?'

'How well do you remember her? The way she looked, I mean.'

The old eyes clouded a little. 'She was always beautiful, that's how I remember her, beautiful and gay.'

A sound like a sob broke from Julie's throat. It was somehow shocking. Mrs Calmady turned her head.

'Julie, was that you? Crying at such a time, when your heart should be overflowing with happiness. Nothing will bring Birdie back, but we have her daughter with us. Oh, my dear, there's so much I want to know, the little things strangers never notice, the tiny things that will bring her back and that I can't hope to hear from anyone else in the world.'

Barbara's voice came faint as a spring wind. 'I'll try and remember. I only wish I had some photographs, but you know nearly everything was lost. There was an accident, oh, it doesn't matter now, I'm all right, but it was a bit shaking, and I feel a bit confused. You mustn't mind if I seem rather muddled. . . .'

'Are you afraid I'll be a nuisance? You shan't tell me anything you don't want to. Only—just one question? Barbara, are you engaged—to be married?'

'No. Oh no. Did anyone give you the impression I was?'

'It doesn't seem possible, a girl like you,' the old woman murmured. 'I'd have known you anywhere for Birdie's daughter. And perhaps there is someone. Only, my darling, be sure, be very, very sure. It's so easy to make a mistake. Women aren't like men, they live for love and marriage, and if that goes wrong you've lost your real life, and we only have one life.' She ended on a note of anguish; she was thinking, as both her listeners

37

appreciated, of Birdie, her heart's darling, who had married wrong and gone into the dark and died there. Any place where there is no love is the dark.

Julie's anger bubbled. She knows nothing, nothing, about her darling Birdie, she thought. I could have told her. Birdie losing her life for love! Not she. Birdie had gone off with Fitton because at the moment he was the one she wanted, but he hadn't been the light of her days. There had been others afterwards, just as there had been others before him. Julie knew. Sometimes she was tempted to say how much she knew, but it wouldn't have been any good, because Mrs Calmady wouldn't have believed her. No, Birdie was Love's martyr, wearing a martyr's crown.

The girl was speaking; she had a voice that would melt a stone. Good girls don't look like that, speak like that. Virtue is its own reward and as a rule its only one. Julie knew suddenly they'd done something terribly dangerous, and it was too late to draw back.

'You mustn't waste your strength being afraid for me,' urged the soft, young voice. 'I shall be all right.'

'How sure you sound! The young are always sure. And the old are arrogant. Arrogant enough to believe they can save the young from suffering. And it isn't true, of course. Nobody can do that.'

'Mother!' Julie came forward. 'Don't get excited, you know what the doctor said. You don't want to overtax your strength.'

'My dear Julie, I'm like someone with five shillings in her purse. She can spend it all at once or eke it out, but whichever way it won't be more than five shillings.'

'Eke it out,' urged the gentle voice. 'I'll be here to-morrow and the day after and the day after that, and for as long as you want me.'

The old woman smiled strangely. 'For the rest of my life. You promise me that, don't you?'

And the girl said, 'I promise.' Her voice was like the sun breaking through a cheerless night.

'Then stay a little longer now. Don't listen to your aunt when she says you're wearing me out. You're like a fount of life to me. You can put the shade on the lamp now, Julie, and I expect you've got lots to do. I take up too much of your time as it is. Now I'm going to shut my eyes and imagine it's Birdie sitting here. I should like to die with the sound of her voice in my ears.'

The dream continued. Now it was superimposed on the face of reality. Barbara Field, that mirage of a few lost days, no longer had any existence. The ghost behind Barbara Field withdrew into the shadows; only Barbara Fitton lived, and as the first week merged into the second and the third loomed on the horizon the girl felt that the only individuality she could look for was Barbara Fitton, that other lost girl who would never return to the world of living men. To be successful with the old lady she must do her best to get into that girl's skin. In the evenings she would pore over the few letters that she had sent, trying to discover what she was like.

'Don't try so hard,' Miles told her. 'You're doing very well as you are.'

'An actress as good as you shouldn't ever be out of a job,' Julie congratulated her sourly. 'Sometimes I can hardly believe you aren't the girl you pretend to be.'

'Then help me,' Barbara pleaded. 'Think of me as your niece.'

But that was asking too much, and both realised it.

'It wouldn't surprise me if the real Barbara Fitton had been a gold-digger,' decided Barbara Fitton's stand-in, looking at herself in the glass. 'You stayed with your father because you thought he could give you a good time.' That much, at all events, emerged from the letters. But the path was fraught with danger.

'Do you never hear from your stepmother?' old Mrs Calmady wanted to know.

'I'm not much of a correspondent,' Barbara excused herself, 'and she's gone back to her own people.'

'If she asks me where that is I'm sunk,' she panicked, but the old lady wasn't interested in the second Mrs Fitton. The first had held all her heart.

Sometimes the enormity of what she was doing almost overwhelmed the girl; she had never dreamed that the doting grandmother would trust her so implicitly. And yet what harm was she really doing? She had no ulterior motive, didn't expect to make anything beyond the initial payment agreed with Miles Calmady. Ah, but she hadn't expected her own heart to be engaged. She had begun to feel for Mrs Calmady the affection and tenderness a granddaughter might have known.

Miles at all events recognised this.

'I haven't a doubt that it was providential for us your reading that advertisement,' he told her. 'You've certainly brought Mrs Calmady more happiness than she's known in years.'

'I'm afraid nearly all the time,' replied Barbara steadily. 'I've only got to make one slip that she notices and the whole situation will collapse like a house of cards.'

'Then you must keep watch and ward and make sure you don't commit any such error,' was his cool reply.

Julie could have helped if she would, with little bits about Birdie as a girl, little stories she might have passed on to a daughter. But Julie stood outside, and wouldn't play.

'Julie was always jealous of Birdie,' Miles explained. 'I was only a child at the time, but even a child couldn't remain indifferent.'

'I can't help feeling sorry for her. It must seem so unfair. To be the elder daughter and see your junior preferred at every turn, for there's no question at all where her mother's preference lay. She couldn't help that, perhaps, but did she have to show it so clearly? There are times when I feel her mother has more affection for me, the imposter, the—the upstart—than she has for her own daughter, who has given Mrs Calmady her life.'

'You've been seeing too many films,' Miles warned her. 'Nobody asked Julie to give up her life. Her mother wasn't always an old lady, and twenty years ago Julie could have done what she pleased with her life.'

'That makes it all the worse, to feel it was all for nothing. I wish she didn't feel she had to regard me as her enemy. I'm here for such a little time. Can't she think of me as a nurse or something like that, someone who's here to soothe her mother's path during her last few weeks? It would be so much easier for me, if she could.'

'I'm afraid it is a hard job for you,' acknowledged Miles, sympathetically, and at that instant Julie came into the room.

'What's this about a hard job?' she demanded in truculent tones. 'What's so hard about it? You're being very comfortably housed and fed, and being paid in addition for doing nothing much that I can see. You don't even have to wash up.'

'That would be simple. I should have some time off then, but as it is I'm on duty twenty-four hours of the day. At any moment Mrs Calmady may want me, even in the middle of the night, and you know how it is when you are awakened suddenly. It takes a few minutes for you to pull yourself together, remember who you are, why you're here. It would be so easy to lose your identity for a moment, and the harm, once done, could never be repaired.'

'Barbara's right, you know,' Miles agreed. 'We're all in this and we must pull together. If any of us three makes a mistake, it would have been better to have told the truth from the start.'

'Which, if you remember, is what I wanted.'

'I know you did, but Dr Stuart said her heart wouldn't stand the shock.'

'It'll be worse if she learns the truth now.'

'Then we shall all have to be careful that she doesn't. It's not for long. . . .'

'We can't be sure of that. Dr Stuart said yesterday that her condition's a miracle, and there's no doubt about it she has a keener grip on life than she had two weeks ago.'

'We have Barbara to thank for that. You should be grateful to her. Don't you want your mother's last few days to be happy ones?'

The look in the woman's eyes was truly terrifying. 'Don't talk to me about what I want for my mother. You've never known anything. Of course I want her to die happy, I've given everything to her—that's what's so intolerable. She doesn't want anything I have to give, she's utterly dependent on a girl who's play-acting for the sake of whatever benefit she can reap for herself out of the situation.'

'No,' cried Barbara, starting forward. 'You've no right . . .'

Miles touched her arm. 'Run up and see if Mrs Calmady wants anything,' he suggested.

'There you are,' cried Julie, almost demented with pain. 'Even you turn to her, in my very presence and say that my mother, my own mother, would rather see her than me. Oh, she's played her cards very cleverly, she's bewitched you all, you and Dr Stuart and Mother. Even Florrie, that half-wit, thinks of her as some angel out of a film. And yet what do we know about her, except that she was ready to deceive an old woman for money? We've got no references, why, we only have her word for it that her father exists, he never writes, and what's more, she never writes to anyone either. Isn't that strange? Oh, I'm not so blind as you suppose, I believe we may have laid a trap and been caught in it ourselves.'

For one shocking moment Barbara was tempted to tell them the truth, but fortunately Miles caught her arm and thrust her from the room.

'Have you taken leave of your senses?' he demanded furiously of Julie. 'Do you want that girl to walk out on us now?'

Julie laughed, a harsh, bitter sound. 'Don't worry, she won't. She knows which side her bread's buttered. But for a man with a responsible job you seem to me remarkably obtuse. Don't you see, when it's all over, she's got us in the palm of her hand? She can either claim Barbara Fitton's inheritance or exact payment for keeping her mouth shut. Oh, I don't say she could get the money, but she could make your position remarkably unpleasant, and mine, too, of course, only no one ever thinks of that. . . . Mind you, she hasn't a thing among her possessions to support any claim she might make. . . .'

'We don't know what she has among her possessions,' returned Miles, sharply.

'I do. Oh, there's no need to look like that, I have some sense of responsibility if you have gone completely haywire over a pretty face. How do we know who we've admitted into the house? She might be a member of a gang. . . .'

'Who knew we were going to advertise? Julie, you don't really mean you've been through her things?'

'Yes, I do, and I'll tell you something. There's absolutely nothing to show that Barbara Field is even her right name. She hasn't asked you to stamp her insurance card since she came, has she?'

'As Barbara Fitton, on a visit, she wouldn't need one.'

'She's not Barbara Fitton, and as Barbara Field she must have had one. But she hasn't. She's got no personal papers at all. Doesn't that strike you as odd?'

'Not nearly so odd as you going through her things. Anyway, she probably carries them about with her in her bag. I suppose you haven't searched that?'

'Yes, I have.'

'Julie!'

'Someone has to think of Mother. Is it natural that a girl with looks like that would take on this sort of job unless she expects to make something out of it? Of course it isn't. I tell you, Miles, I don't trust her. I hate leaving her alone with Mother. How do we know what she may not try and worm out of her?'

'She's absolutely powerless, and you know it. Your mother's will . . .'

'People can change wills, can't they? But it isn't money I'm thinking of. Not an hour ago Mother asked me to give her her jewel-case. She hasn't asked for that for months. I don't know if you've ever seen it open. She's got some lovely things Father gave her. She's probably going through them now, and you've sent that girl up there. . . .'

'Barbara didn't know she had the jewel-case.'

'How can you say that? We don't know what she knew. Why, she probably led the conversation round to jewels. You know how Mother adores talking about the past. All Barbara has to do is egg her on—You must have looked lovely in the diamonds, I wish I could have seen you—it would be as simple as that. I dare say she can't get money out of Mother, though I wouldn't put that past her, but jewels are different.'

'If your mother gives her something, believing her to be Barbara Fitton, it wouldn't hold good in a court of law, even if she tried to hold on to them, and I don't believe she would.'

'A court of law,' repeated Julie scornfully. 'Who's going to take it that far? Are you going to stand up and declare publicly that you engaged a tuppenny-ha'penny actress, about whom you know nothing whatsoever, remember that, to pretend to be a dead girl? Of course not. It would ruin you. Why, the first suggestion would be that it was a put-up trick between you. That she knew the advertisement was going to appear, that she'd answer it and you'd pick out her application from all the others. And every scrap of evidence would support it. In fact,' she stared, 'it's even possible that's the truth.'

Disregarding his exclamation of, 'Don't be absurd, Julie!' she went on: 'I thought at the time it was odd, that you didn't even consider anyone else. . . .'

'You want to be careful,' he warned her, 'or you'll start believing the truth of what you say.'

'Why shouldn't it be true?' she demanded excitedly. 'You waived the question of references, you insisted on bringing her into the house in almost indecent haste. If she's really the person she claims to be why hasn't she produced a lawyer or a doctor or a clergyman to vouch for her.'

'Because time was the essence of the affair, you know that as well as I do. And you must allow me some intuition—or is that the monopoly of your sex?'

He was getting angry and her own miserable suspicions were strengthened thereby.

'Is there a tie-up between you?' she demanded. 'Perhaps she's working on Mother to make you her heir, seeing Birdie and Birdie's daughter are both gone.'

'Your mother doesn't know that Barbara Fitton's dead.'

'But Barbara Field does. I'm going up this minute. . . .'

'No!' But she shook off his restraining arm.

'How dare you try to stop me? Perhaps you even suggested Mother should ask for her jewel-box. Perhaps you said how nice Barbara would look. . . .'

'You're out of your mind, Julie. I repeat, whatever your mother gave her she couldn't keep it.'

'Is that your intuition again? Well, mine tells me she both

could and would. And there at least I shouldn't blame her. There isn't a natural woman living who would say 'No' to jewels if they came her way. And why should she?'

'Why should you mind so much if your mother does give her something?' he asked curiously. 'What she's doing for us is worth far more than the fifty pounds we're paying her. A brooch or a bracelet would be a little thing.'

'So you are behind her? Why didn't I realise that from the start? I'm going up this minute.' She sprang for the stairs. 'No, Julie.'

'You can't stop me. I'm going to tell Mother I've only just discovered the truth, that this girl's an impostor. She may be brazen, but I'd like to see her brazen her way out of this.'

But as she began to race up the stairs, with Miles at her heels, Barbara appeared at the head of the stairway. She looked pale and distressed.

'I was just coming to look for you,' she said. 'Mrs Calmady wants you both.'

Julie pushed past her into the old woman's room, thrusting against the girl with such violence that she stumbled, and might have fallen but for Miles's restraining arm.

'What's wrong?' he asked.

'It's getting too much for me,' she said. 'I never thought I was going to grow fond of her or she of me. I don't think I can go on deceiving her much longer.'

Mrs Calmady was looking pleased and rather excited. Her eyes were bright, there was even a little colour in the thin cheeks. At the sight of the bed Miles uttered an involuntary exclamation. The pale satin quilt was covered with precious stones, rubies and diamonds and emeralds, all winking in the daylight.

'It's a good thing you don't let the world know what you've got,' he rallied her. 'You're temptation personified to a gang.'

'Henry never had much opinion of money as such,' said Mrs Calmady placidly. 'He said it was an undependable quantity. You could never be sure when it would lose its value, and while it was in the bank you got no pleasure from it, beyond the knowledge that it was there. He was a demon for work and he

45

ANTHONY GILBERT

liked to see the results of his labours—a house or a motor car or jewellery. It's an odd thing,' continued the old woman, her eyes brightening still more at the recollection of that rich past, 'I sometimes thought he cared more for jewels than I did myself. It was the colours, I believe. Perhaps he was an artist *manqué*— his working life was as drab as most working lives are. And, of course, he liked to see me wear them. Not that I've worn them much since his death. I used to dream of seeing Birdie in them; she was to take what she wanted, because so many of them are only suitable to the young, and she was the kind that's born to wear beauty.'

'Not like me,' agreed Julie in a grating voice. 'You never thought of giving me any in your lifetime, did you, Mother?'

'My dear, they'll practically all come to you when I'm gone. But there are too many for any one person, and besides, when could you wear them in this quiet country life? We got out so little. It's an odd thing, Julie,' she added in a surprised tone, 'I've never thought of you as caring about jewellery.'

'No,' agreed her daughter in the same embittered voice, as though she were suffocating and the words only shaped themselves with appalling difficulty, 'I don't believe you've ever thought of me as a woman at all. It was always Birdie from the time we were girls, Birdie to have the lovely clothes, Birdie to go to parties, with the side door left on the latch, because Father had odd ideas about a daughter's honour. . . .'

'Julie!' That was Miles. He caught his cousin's arm in a savage grip. She shook it off as if it were a beetle or some chance wandering fly.

'Why shouldn't we have a little truth before the end? You've always idolised Birdie,' she accused her mother. 'You never let yourself believe she was as hard as nails. Oh yes, she was. Nobody ever mattered to her but Birdie. Look at the way she ran off with that scoundrel. She knew it would break your heart, but did she care? Of course she didn't.'

Mrs Calmady turned to the shaking girl. 'You mustn't listen to her, she was always jealous of your mother, and perhaps she's right, perhaps it was partly my fault, but there was something so gay, so radiant about her. You can't help loving the sun

46

when you see it, can you? And now you've brought the sun back into my sky. I want to give myself the pleasure of giving you something while I can still do it in person. Come here, my dear.'

Ashen-faced, the girl came closer to the bed.

'I'm going to be very candid,' the old woman went on. 'You mustn't mind. Old age must have its liberties, when it has so little else. When I got your letter saying you were going to stay in Canada until you'd graduated, I began to be convinced you never meant to come. I tried to accept the disappointment, though how keen that was you will never guess, keener than a surgeon's knife to me. Indeed, I would have submitted to any operation if, in return, I could see you before I died. I even tried to make a bargain. Let Birdie's daughter come back before I die and you can exact any price you like, I prayed. But, of course, you can't bargain with God. And then, when I'd almost given up hope, you came, and you were everything I'd dreamed, and more—oh, much more.' The old veined hands moved among the jewels, selected a necklace of pearls, beautifully graded and fitted with a little diamond clasp, added a pair of ear-rings and a ring of pearls set with small diamonds. 'These were meant for your mother on her wedding day, but she never had a wedding under my roof. When I knew what had happened I wanted to send them after her, but your grandfather wouldn't let me. It's a dreadful thing to say of the dead, but I don't think he ever quite forgave Birdie for that. Did she ever speak of him, say he was a tyrant?'

Barbara shook her head. She was beyond speech; this was the moment she had feared, when her heart was so deeply engaged she couldn't answer for her own control.

'I'm glad of that, because it wasn't true. But he'd been so proud of her, he never thought anyone quite good enough. Perhaps we were wrong, we didn't understand how to deal with her. Perhaps the older generation is always wrong, trying to use its own yardstick to measure the needs of the generation ahead. She must have loved your father very much to do what she did, give up so much, and it didn't last. That's what breaks my heart, that it didn't last.'

47

'Stop this, Mother,' cried Julie. 'You don't understand.'

'Isn't that what I'm saying? Anyway, don't look back, never look back. There's the present for us all and for you, my darling, the future, too. So I want you to have these now.' She gathered the pearls in the palms of her thin old hands and held them out to the girl.

Barbara stood like a stone. 'No,' she whispered at last. 'No, I can't.'

'Of course you can. I'm so glad I thought of this. My dear, you won't know this side of Paradise what you've done for me. I had so many fears that Birdie's child might disappoint me, and they were all misplaced. You've made these last weeks so radiant—I swear to you that if the impossible should happen and it could be proved that you weren't Birdie's daughter at all, but some stranger come out of the street to be with me at the end, I should still want you to have them. Doesn't that satisfy you?'

To her horror Barbara found her eyes brimming with tears. She came forward, at a gentle push from Miles, and took the pearls in silence.

'Put them on,' the old woman pleaded. 'They look dull now, of course. Pearls need to be worn if they're to stay lustrous. And they should be worn by the young, they need the vitality of youth. Miles, fasten the necklace for her. Why, child, your hands are shaking.'

Miles dropped Julie's arm that he had been holding all this while and took the pearls from the girl's hand. As he fastened them round her throat she slipped the ring on her finger, and took up the ear-rings.

'Why, they're for pierced ears,' she discovered.

'Your mother had hers pierced. You must remember . . .'

'Yes,' murmured the girl, in confusion, but now Julie leaped forward, her voice breaking like a clap of thunder to fill the room with sound and fury.

'Of course she doesn't remember, she doesn't know anything about her, she never set eyes on Birdie, she was never in Canada. She's what you called her an instant ago, a stranger from the street come in to deceive you into believing she had a right here.' Her breath choked her. Mrs Calmady's face had gone as white as the pearls. Barbara stood staring at the earrings in her hand, oblivious to the ring shining on her finger.

'What on earth has come over you, Julie? Of course, this is Birdie's daughter. . . .'

'Ask Miles, if you don't believe me. After all, it was his plan.'

Old Mrs Calmady turned her puzzled eyes on the girl, who now lifted her own. 'Forgive me,' they implored, 'forgive me.' 'It can't be true,' the old woman whispered, 'you wouldn't do that.'

Even now Miles would have tried to retrieve the day, but it was too late. Barbara was speaking.

'It's all true, it's absolutely true, and it's wrong, I should never have agreed. We hoped you need never know.'

'Are you telling me you are not Birdie's daughter?'

'Yes. It's too late to deceive you any longer. Selfishly, I'm relieved you should know the truth. We didn't mean you ever to know. You mustn't blame Miles, he meant it for the best, he wanted you to die happy.'

'So she didn't come, after all.' All the light was gone from the eyes, the warmth from the fading voice.

'She did, she did, but—it was true about the accident, and nobody had the heart to tell you. They thought if only you could believe she had come, and she did mean to, she set out, but the plane crashed. And Miles thought if I could act as—as her stand-in, as it were. . . .'

'Where did he find you?'

'Through an advertisement. I answered it before I had any idea what it involved. If I'd known I should never have dared. But I—I was in a bit of trouble myself, I wanted to make a fresh start, and it seemed providential, Barbara being my name, too. I never guessed I was going to come to love you. I've hated it so, cheating you all this time. Try to believe that, because that at least is true.'

'You see what a good actress she is,' broke in Julie's savage voice. 'I can't think how we managed to get her, a girl like that shouldn't have any trouble finding parts. But perhaps the trouble was with the police,' she wound up, cruelly.

Barbara flinched. 'Why should you say that?'

'Don't suppose we believe your story about your father marrying again. It was just one more lie along with the rest. Now we're having a showdown let's have some facts. Was it the police?'

'There's no need for Barbara to answer any of your questions,' put in Miles icily. 'Her affairs are her own concern. From our point of view her life began the day she came here. And don't think I blame you,' he added to the girl, 'you did what we asked and you did it far better than any of us dared to hope. Stuart himself told me you'd brought my aunt a new lease of life.'

'If you weren't afraid of the police, who were you afraid of?' Julie wasn't to be silenced.

'Afraid I shouldn't be successful, of course, that one day you'd find me out. Oh, I don't mean you'd ever try to trip me up,' she was talking to the old woman now, 'for why should you suppose I wasn't honest and genuine?'

'Honest!' hooted Julie. 'It amazes me to know you've ever heard the word. You're just a charlatan.'

'Be quiet!' The old woman's voice startled them all with its authoritative note. 'I'm certain you're wrong. Oh, not about this not being Birdie's daughter. Barbara herself admits that, but that she was a charlatan, no, that at least is a lie. You talk as if it were easy to hoodwink the old, because they're dull-witted and half-blind, to all intents and purposes moribund. But, as your bodily functions fail, you develop a more acute spiritual sense, which enables you to distinguish between love and its counterfeit. Do you know what has surprised me most during these past weeks—it is that Birdie's daughter should offer me a disinterested affection. I hadn't expected that, it was like a miracle. You taunted me just now, Julie, with not knowing what Birdie was like. You're wrong, I did know, I've known for nearly twenty years, but I wouldn't let myself believe it, because I had so little left if I let that go. And when I heard her daughter was here I warned myself not to pitch my hopes too high. She'd come, I said. Wasn't that enough? And then it was borne in on me that everything she did for me was done, not because of what she hoped to get out of it, but because, as she said, she did really love me. I don't know what arrangement you made with her, Miles, but a thousand pounds wouldn't buy the tenderness, the goodness she had shown me. And from a girl who could expect nothing in return. It's more than I had any right to look for, that at the end of my days I should be crowned.' Her voice died away; no one else dared speak. When she uttered again it was on a lower, slower note. 'Miles, it's true about Barbara Fitton?'

'I'm afraid it is. We made every possible inquiry. She was on board. There were no survivors.'

'Then to-morrow will you get Mr Cutbush to come down? I want to add a codicil to my will. And tell him not to delay. I have the feeling there isn't very much time left.'

CHAPTER 4

Miles Calmady was telephoning from the extension in the library. He hung up the receiver and came into the big room that had been called the drawing-room in the days when people had such luxuries, to say thoughtfully to his cousin, 'I don't think Aunt May is going to be very pleased about this. Cutbush is laid up with 'flu, won't be allowed out of bed for two or three days and certainly won't be allowed to go traipsing round the countryside inside of a week. One of the partners is coming in his place, a chap called Menzies. I don't think any of us know him: but it seemed better to agree to that than to chance Cutbush being able to get down in time.'

'Is there really so much hurry?' Julie demanded belligerently.

'Your mother thinks so, and she's the person to be considered. Mind you, I don't say there wouldn't be time, but I'm not prepared to take the risk. Besides, Aunt May's worked herself up about this, and she won't settle till the affair's been dealt with.'

'And of course Barbara supports her? How that creature has pulled wool over all your eyes, except mine. For a man who's supposed to have some experience of life, Miles, I must say I'm surprised at you.'

'Why supposed?' he asked coolly. 'I have experience.'

'And yet you're prepared to stand by and see me disinherited in favour of that little cheat, that adventuress. . . .'

'That's actionable. And there's no question of your being dispossessed, and well you know it. Your mother's a comparatively wealthy woman and you'll be left very comfortably off.

If she chooses to leave Barbara a small legacy, surely that's her affair.'

'You don't get a lawyer down from London for a small legacy,' retorted Julie shrewdly. 'You draw a cheque. No, she means to put her in Birdie's place at my expense. I warn you, I shall contest the will.'

'You'll be a great fool, if you do. You'll not only have me and the doctor against you, you'll have public opinion as well. You'll appear in the unattractive rôle of the middle-aged woman who grudges a girl a little reward for what's been a very tough assignment. No, do try and be reasonable, my dear. Menzies won't allow her to do anything desperate, and to do her justice, I don't think Aunt May has anything extravagant in mind.'

'Then you know Mother even less well than I thought. She's absolutely sold on Barbara Field, if that really is her name. Look at the way she handed her the pearls. Not that she's going to keep them.'

'She'll be a great fool if she gives them up, and I don't for a moment suppose she will. Why should she? They were given her in the full knowledge of her identity, and in the presence of two witnesses.'

'She had no right to do anything of the sort,' Julie insisted. 'Now Birdie and Birdie's daughter are gone they're mine. Mr Cutbush was such a fool Mother could twist him round her little finger; let's hope this Mr Menzies has more sense. I shall make a point of having a word with him. Why, for all we know, Barbara makes a profession of attending sick old women's death-beds.'

'And drawing handsome legacies? My dear Julie, where's your sense of proportion. If that's her line why isn't she living on her ill-gotten gains instead of working here twenty-four hours out of twenty-four? Oh yes, she is. She's been up in the night more often than not. Now do try and calm down. I assure you Menzies won't let her do anything unreasonable.'

'How can he prevent her? A lawyer's job is to take his client's instructions.'

'And offer advice. I shall meet him at the station and put him in the picture. As a matter of fact, if the truth should come out, the people who will be censured will be our two selves, for starting up this game in the first place.'

Robert Menzies was considerably younger than Miles had, perhaps illogically, anticipated. When he saw a tall stranger, with auburn hair and eyes as blue as old Mrs Calmady's had once been, swing off the train, he did not at first realise that this was the man he had come to meet. Indeed, it was Menzies who made the first approach.

'Mr Calmady?'

'Yes. And you . . .'

'I'm Menzies. Good of you to meet me. I hope it wasn't inconvenient.'

Privately Miles had sometimes wondered why his aunt had stayed with her London firm of solicitors, seeing she had left the capital nearly twenty years before, but she had summoned them so seldom and had at one time leaped at the excuse of going to London to consult them, and naturally lawyers don't like losing clients any more than anyone else.

'Not at all. All the effort's on your part. I thought I'd take this opportunity of explaining the rather unconventional situation you're going to find up at the house. I've got my car here. . . .'

If Menzies would have employed a stronger term than unconventional to describe the position, he kept his opinion to himself, preserving a poker face while the astounding story was unfolded to him.

'I suppose, as a lawyer, you take everything in your stride,' commented Miles, slightly ruffled by this surface composure. 'Though I imagine you don't often come across a story as original as this.'

'Original?' Menzies laughed for the first time. 'Why, it's the oldest of old hats. When I was a boy I used to stay with an aunt in the country during my school holidays, and she had an immense collection of ancient magazines, bought to beguile her on her endless railway journeys, and this was the plot of at least one yarn in five. Of course, the details differed in each case, but the outlines were similar. Usually two girls met in a railway carriage, one a pauper looking for a job, some form of slave labour as she was never trained for anything professional, and the other an heiress from Canada or South Africa, it didn't really matter which so long as the relations she was coming to meet had never been in either. During the journey the rich girl had a heart attack and died quietly in the carriage, having thoughtfully told her story in practically every detail to her companion. This was the opportunity for Little Orphan Annie to take over her luggage, personal papers and identity before she pulled the communication cord. Of course, there was always a snag. Either a young man blew in who, for some mysterious reason, had been overlooked by the dead girl, and hailed the impostor as Cynthia or Myra or whatever name she'd adopted, at the same time saluting her with an affectionate kiss. Or the other version contained a smiling villain who was heir to the dead girl's fortune, and spent the rest of the story trying to put her out of the way.'

'And in that version,' countered Miles pleasantly, 'the young man appears a little later, and saves the heroine in the approved manner.'

'I see you know the ropes,' Menzies congratulated him. 'All the same, as the family lawyer, I must point out you were taking a whale of a risk. You don't appear to know anything about this girl except what she's chosen to tell you.'

'What else would you expect me to know?' asked Miles reasonably. 'If she'd been a personal acquaintance we couldn't have put the plot into action at all. Yes, of course it was a risk, but so was telling my aunt the truth, and in my opinion a greater one. As it happens, everything's turned out well.'

But the young lawyer still frowned. 'I can't see that there'd be any harm in verifying Miss Field's statements. From what you've told me, I gather Mrs Calmady intends to do something handsome for her.'

'No one could grudge Barbara that,' Miles assured him quickly. 'If you'd been in the house during the past month you'd appreciate the situation better. It's like falling in love at first sight, you're up to your neck before you know where you are. And in fact that's not a bad simile. Aunt May fell for the girl on the spot, and I think Barbara reciprocated. She can't have anticipated that she'd get anything out of it beyond the agreed payment. When you've met her,' he added comfortably, 'you'll understand what I mean.'

'I only hope you don't over-estimate my powers of comprehension. To be frank with you, Calmady, the whole thing sounds screwy to me, and I feel Mr Cutbush will take the same view.'

Julie was waiting in the hall when they arrived, wearing her hat and coat. 'I'm going down to the village,' she announced abruptly. 'Mother's suddenly thought of some things she must have and it's early closing day. Of course, this is really Barbara's job, but she went off on the bus to Beachampton directly after breakfast, and goodness knows when she'll be back.'

Miles effected the necessary introductions as soon as he could get a word in edgewise.

'Don't let my mother get over-excited,' Julie told the young man in her ungracious fashion. 'She's worked up enough about this. I only hope, as an unprejudiced person, you'll prevent her doing anything too crazy. I'm afraid I don't share my cousin's faith in Miss Field's blameless motives.'

She jerked her head in farewell and went away. Miles was looking uncomfortable.

'Julie's jealous,' he said simply. 'I suppose it's not altogether surprising. But I don't for a moment believe my aunt means to worsen her situation by any legacy she intends leaving to Miss Field.'

Menzies's first impression of his client was of a quite extraordinary charm. Old Mrs Calmady's eyes were bright, her cheeks pink; she greeted him with an old-world formality that at the same time bade him welcome. He found himself thinking the deceased Calmady must have been a boor of the first water to account for Julie's manner and unprepossessing appearance.

'I do hope my daughter hasn't alarmed you,' she said, as Miles left them together. 'It's true that I'm in frail health, but I know exactly what I have in mind, and I shan't detain you very long.'

Clients always said that, the young man reflected, but here

for a wonder was one who fulfilled her promise. He drew up the codicil according to her instructions and read it over to her.

'Miss Field's a very lucky young woman,' he observed.

'Oh no,' said Mrs Calmady decidedly. 'It's I who am lucky. When you're my age death has lost a lot of its powers, or perhaps it would be truer to say that life has lost a good deal of its hold. I was quite ready to go once I'd set eyes on my granddaughter, but since Barbara's arrival I find I want to hold on as long as I can. It's what they call an Indian summer, isn't it? I do hope you can stay to lunch, then you'll see her. It was like her delicacy to suggest going into Beachampton this morning.'

Presently she asked him to sound the electric bell that stood at her elbow.

'I call that my mythical Belinda,' she told him, smiling. 'I can reach it with practically no exertion at all, and the instant it sounds someone, generally Barbara, comes running. Even if it's the middle of the night she hears it, and she's made me promise to ring if I want her no matter what the hour. And of course it is a relief to feel you're not a burden twenty-four hours a day, as I should be if I had to have someone always with me. Though I suppose the young will never realise it, old people do sometimes enjoy their own company.'

He thought she was one of the most charming old ladies he had ever met. When their business was complete, she told Florrie to fetch the sherry decanter.

'It's not often I take stimulants, other than what the doctor orders,' she confided, 'but this is a very special occasion. And when you see my nephew, be sure to tell him I'm not in the least exhausted, only very, very happy that everything's settled. This was the last thing I had to worry over this side the grave. Do you read Lord Tennyson? I'm told he's out of date, like everything else that was fashionable when I was a girl. There was a poem of his:

> Sunset and evening bell,
> And after that the dark,
> And may there be no sadness of farewell
> When I embark.

That's how I hope it'll be for me, too.'

Julie had just returned when he came down into the hall. 'It's all done, Miss Calmady,' he told her. 'I don't think your mother's at all upset. She knew her own mind, and that's more than half the battle.'

'Battle! What an extraordinary word to use.' She looked at him out of those piercing brown eyes. 'Do you really think she's in a fit state to change her will?'

'If all our clients were as balanced as Mrs Calmady our lives would be far simpler,' he told her. 'We had a very easy interview, and everything's settled. A codicil's not a very involved affair at any time, and once it's drawn up there's nothing to be added except a signature, and then you can put the whole affair out of mind.'

She sent him a look of such contemptuous hatred that at first he couldn't believe his eyes. Then, without another word, she went upstairs, and he turned into the drawing-room.

'All set?' murmured Miles.

'I shan't need to trouble her again. It was all very simple.'

'You'll stay to lunch, of course, and meet the lucky legatee. How about a drink?'

'I've already had an excellent glass of sherry with your aunt.'

Miles's eyebrows lifted. 'Did you, b'Jove? I hope Stuart won't make trouble over that. She never takes wine as a rule.'

'She regarded this as a kind of celebration.'

'Oh well,' agreed Miles, 'I dare say one glass won't hurt her.'

The telephone rang and he went across the hall into the library to answer it. It was from his office, that he had deserted for once, on his aunt's behalf. A ticklish piece of business had come up, and, as he might have expected, they'd botched it. Trying to unravel the threads and promising to come in after lunch, he forgot all about Mrs Calmady and her codicil.

Julie hurried up the stairs, tossed her hat and coat on to the bed, and went unceremoniously into her mother's room. Old Mrs Calmady wore an expression her daughter had seldom seen of late years, a look of utter peace and satisfaction. But it was more than that. There was a serene gaiety about her that was new; now she was past the troubles and turmoils of life and awaited the close with tranquillity.

'You've been drinking sherry,' Julie accused her, seeing the decanter and the two glasses. 'I knew something fatal would happen if I left you alone with that young man.'

'My dear Julie,' said her mother in decided tones, 'do please realise you're not a member of the Gestapo. If I choose to have a glass of sherry with a charming young man I am surely old enough to please myself.'

'Dr Stuart wouldn't approve. Is he staying to lunch?'

'Mr Menzies? I hope so. I want him to meet Barbara.'

Julie's brows drew together forbiddingly. 'Did he let you execute the codicil?'

'Let me? There was no question of getting his permission. He drew up the codicil I dictated, and . . .'

'I think it's only right to tell you that I shall dispute it,' Julie interrupted. 'I shall claim undue influence. Oh, yes I shall. It's perfectly obvious to us all that you're completely under that girl's thumb. But it may not sound so good when the whole truth comes out, that she came here under false pretences.'

'Aided and abetted by my daughter and my nephew.'

'I couldn't stand against Miles, and you know it, though if I'd realised at the time that it was nothing but a plot . . .'

She paused and Mrs Calmady looked perplexed. 'I can't understand what you mean by that, my dear. You knew it was a plot, if you insist on employing that melodramatic expression.'

'Ah, but I didn't know the whole. It never passed through my mind that Miles knew Barbara before he brought her here.'

'Who says he did? He got her through an advertisement.'

Julie laughed, a jangling, discordant sound. 'That's what he told you. Doesn't it strike you as odd that he never considered any of the other letters, simply picked hers out and brought her here without even consulting me? Of course, I realised too late it was a put-up job between them. She knew the advertisement would be in the paper, she was to answer it and he was to go through the formality of inviting her for an interview.'

59

'I never heard anything sillier in my life,' declared Mrs Calmady, but a faint note of panic sounded in the old voice. 'He could perfectly well have introduced her as Barbara Field. He didn't have to pretend she was my granddaughter.'

'Ah, but you wouldn't be likely to make Barbara Field a legatee, while Miles can't hope to benefit much from your will, being only a nephew by marriage, if he is your executor. No, no, they played their hands very cleverly. Did you know he stole all Birdie's letters and gave them to this girl to learn by heart? I've heard them rehearsing over and over again in the evening the sort of things they think you'd like to hear. They're false, false, and scheming, and that's the girl you're going to make an heiress. Are you surprised I should contest the wall?'

'You're talking a lot of nonsense,' protested the old woman, but now the colour had faded from the thin cheeks, the fire died out of the voice; she was just a desperately old, tired and frightened creature, turning her gaze this way and that in a despairing search for peace.

Julie's heart was shut to pity. She came closer to the bed and stared at the trembling face.

'It's worse than you think. The moment you've signed that codicil you've signed your death-warrant. This is all they've been waiting for. Get that into your head. Mind you, you were never meant to know the truth, but I couldn't endure it any longer, all that whispering and lying. But even when you knew she was only a little upstart from the gutter. . . .'

'No!' Painfully the old woman pulled herself more upright in the bed. 'You shan't speak of her like that. It's not true. I shall never believe she only came here with the thought of personal gain. She was so kind, so good . . .'

'Such a good actress you mean,' cried Julie scornfully. 'Oh yes, she played her hand like a master—or should I say a mistress? And all the time she and Miles—did you never guess?'

Now the hectic colour had come back to the thin cheeks. 'I don't know what you wish to imply, Julie, but I don't believe a word of evil against that girl. And I don't think you should be exciting me like this. I shall have one of my attacks. . . .'

She stretched out her hand towards the bell, but Julie was too quick for her; in a trice she had pushed the bell out of reach.

'You *shall* listen,' she insisted fiercely, 'before it's too late. Miles . . .'

'If you're trying to tell me Miles is in love with her, of course I knew it; and who could blame him? The fact is, Julie, you're jealous. You're like a wicked child, you can't have everything you want and you don't see why anybody else should have it. You were just the same with Birdie in the old days. . . .'

Julie's face seemed to contract. She flung up her clenched hands.

'And do you think you weren't to blame then? Sometimes I used to wonder if I was even a human being in the same sense as Birdie was.'

'That's absurd. I always tried to treat you both alike, but you wouldn't be loved, you wouldn't.'

'As if you ever tried! Ho! ho! You never even expected me to have the normal hopes and desires of a girl. Someone must be at your side to make herself useful, the unpaid slave, the one no one notices, Julie can do this, Julie can do that, Julie can stay at home, she won't mind, after all, she's awkward, she doesn't attract men. Did you really suppose I never knew how you felt about me? How everyone felt? You never thought of me as a human being and so gradually I ceased to be one. I became one enormous debit account, item after item, all debits. Even after Birdie married and went abroad you didn't change, though I thought perhaps then you might turn to me as a—as a daughter. But no, I was your cross, crosses have to be borne— did you ever think you can cling even to a cross? Oh, you clung all right, and I accepted it all, all, year after year, till this girl came, laughing and deceitful, pulling the wool over your eyes, saying to Miles. "Be patient, it won't be much longer. One of these days she'll have an attack when she's alone, and her hands shake so she'll never be able to give herself the drops. So—be patient." '

Old Mrs Calmady's eyes were starting out of her head; she was shaking as though she had an ague.

'Go away,' she panted, 'go away before you kill me. I don't

believe a word of it—do you understand, not a word?'

'Of course not. You'd never believe anything against them, dear Miles and sweet little Barbara—sweet, sweet little snake. Did you tell her how much she's to get? I hope she won't be disappointed. Not that it'll matter, because she'll never have a penny. I'm going to see to that—do you understand? Do you?'

She bowed herself over the stricken woman, her eyes burning as if with fever. The old voice had sunk to a breath, a faint air just puffing between the cold lips.

'Get Barbara for me—I want Barbara. I feel ill. . . .'

'Another attack, I suppose. Nonsense, that's just hysteria. For once you shall listen to what I have to say. Yes, isn't that odd? For once I'm the centre of the stage. All these years it's been you in the heart of the picture with people standing round you . . . It's not fair really to blame Birdie for being self-centred. You might as well blame the child of red-haired parents for having Titian hair.'

Now it seemed as if there was a third presence in the room. Death had slipped in while they spoke, stood beside the bed; you could even feel the chill emanating from his breath. Mrs Calmady gave a loud shudder.

'Julie! My drops. Quickly. And fetch Barbara—fetch Barbara.'

'Why should I give them to you? To give you sufficient strength to sign away my inheritance to an adventuress? Wouldn't that be a silly thing for me to do? Well, wouldn't it? Can't you answer me?'

'The drops,' panted the dying voice. 'The drops.'

'All right, I'm getting them. Look, here they are. No, don't snatch. You'll only upset them. See, I'm taking out the cork. Now—I'm putting them in your hand. Hold them steady. You don't want them to upset over the sheet, do you? Just hold it like that while I get some water.' She picked up a tumbler, held it up to the light, fussed and t'cha'ed, then decided the water wasn't altogether fresh, she would refill the glass. And all the time that frail life-giving tube trembled and tilted dangerously in the shaking old hand. But Mrs Calmady made no more pleas. She had no breath to spare for one thing, and for another, she knew it would be fruitless, even if she had. At last Julie came back. 'Barbara should be more careful,' she scolded. 'That water wasn't fresh, there was dust in it. You could swallow a germ. Now then, are you ready? Why, your hand's shaking. Let me hold your wrist.' The big fierce fingers closed round the fragile bones of old age. 'Now then, tilt it—no, not that way.' Her grip tightened, the old woman whispered in pain, her fingers opened and as Julie stealthily withdrew the glass a few inches, the life-giving drops spilled on to the sheet.

'Now see what you've done,' exclaimed Julie, snatching up the phial and turning it upside down. 'Look, not a single drop left. Now we're in a pretty pickle, because by the time we get hold of Dr Stuart and he can send over a fresh supply, it'll be too late. Won't it? Won't it?' She caught the thin shoulder, leaned down over the convulsed face. 'What's that you're trying to say? Barbara! Always Barbara. Really, it's quite monotonous. Anyway, you know the kind of flibbertigibbet she is, gone off to Beachampton to waste your money. Choosing her trousseau, I wouldn't be surprised. No, it's no good ringing the bell, she isn't here, and even if she were there's nothing she could do now. There's nothing anyone could do.' The implacable hand pushed the bell still farther out of the old woman's reach. She stood looking at that pain-racked face. For all her years of attendance in a sick-room she knew very little. How long, for instance, would the flame of life take to flicker out in such circumstances? Be sure she always has her drops immediately, Stuart had said. Perhaps she should go down and let everyone know what had happened. But, on second thoughts, perhaps not. She straightened herself and once more addressed the half-conscious woman on the bed.

'Don't try and reach the bell,' she cautioned her, 'because it's right out of reach. And don't try to call out, because no one would hear. Just lie still, quite, quite still. Really, there's nothing else for you to do.'

The dying woman made no sound; the room was darkening fast, voices were no longer audible; she had suddenly parted company with the gay old lady who had chaffed Robert

Menzies and insisted on drinking a glass of sherry with him.
Only, like a pinpoint of light, gleamed the thought of Barbara;
she clung to that, as she clung to life itself.

CHAPTER 5

It had been Barbara's own suggestion that she should spend the morning in Beachampton, ostensibly to do some necessary shopping, but actually to be off the premises when the lawyer arrived. She was under no illusion as to Julie's view of the proceedings, and though Miles assured her she had earned anything she might subsequently receive, she had the wit to know that to a good many people, possibly Menzies among them, she must seem like a girl who knew which side her bread was buttered and didn't mean it to fall, butter side down, on the carpet. She caught the bus that brought her to Preston at 12.30 and walked happily up to the house, with parcels in her hands and flowers for the old lady and a jar of ginger for Julie, whose pet delicacy it was. She could hear Miles talking in the library, so she turned into the drawing-room to dis-embarrass herself of her parcels. She had wondered if she would find Julie here, but the only occupant was a tall young man with auburn hair who was standing with his hands in his pockets, staring out of the long windows that looked over the lawn.

Barbara came forward, putting down her parcels on the table.

'I suppose you're Mr Menzies,' she said. 'I hope I haven't come back too early. I thought most likely you'd be through before now.'

She was smiling a little, but looking a little anxious, too. He thought he understood the reason for that anxiety.

'I'm sure you did,' he said, taking his hands out of his pockets. 'Otherwise it would have been perfectly simple to stay and lunch in Beachampton. Does it surprise you to know that I was invited to remain simply for the pleasure of meeting you?'

'Well, at least you know who I am,' she smiled back.

'Yes,' he agreed. 'I know. And I could even make a pretty accurate guess as to why you're masquerading here as Barbara Field.'

'Masquerading? Oh, Miles has told you, of course.'

'He's told me as much as he knew. To be fair, I dare say he couldn't tell me more.'

She had stopped smiling; instead she frowned. 'But there is no more—at least . . . ' Naturally, she hadn't told the Calmadys about the loss of memory.

'No more about Barbara Field, you mean? Oh, I can believe that. But—in the course of your conversation did you ever happen to mention Barbara Hurst?'

'Barbara Hurst.' She repeated the name softly. 'Oh—do you mean that's my name?' Sudden excitement fired her; her beauty, that she carried as gently as a bride carries her bouquet, was suddenly as brilliant as an army splendid with banners. 'You mean, you know me? That we've met before? Oh, that's wonderful! Wonderful! This is what I've been waiting for ever since I came here.'

He said, with a tinge of genuine admiration, 'You do it most awfully well. It's no wonder Calmady was deceived. But remember, I'm the professional. You don't have to pull out the stops for me.'

At once the pleasure and the anticipation fled from her face. 'What did that mean? Is there any reason why I shouldn't be glad to know my own name?'

'A case of loss of memory?' he prompted.

'Just that.'

He nodded. 'Could it have happened at a more convenient time? And in, shall we say, three months—or four—it would have found its way home? Well? Am I right?'

She pushed the flowers away from her and they fell to the ground; she stooped with a feeling of guilt, they had been bought with love, now one of the heads was broken. . . .

'Is it any use my saying I don't know what you're talking about?'

He crossed the room and pulled open the door. Miles's

voice could be heard speaking on the telephone. He came back into the room.

'No one's going to overhear us,' he said. 'And you must realise the inadequacy of putting on an act for me. You're a very rash young woman, Barbara Hurst. Did you never hear of George Joseph Smith?'

'I don't think so. Does that make me an ignoramus?'

'He was hanged for murder in 1915. He had a scheme; he married women for what he could get out of them; several of his wives died immediately after making wills from which he benefited. They all died in the same way—drowned in baths. He was always out of the house at the time, shopping. The inquest always took place at the shortest possible notice, generally at a week-end when relatives couldn't get to the scene; the funerals were what you might call economical. The first time this happened everyone was sorry for Mr Smith. A shocking thing to happen. Poor chap! After three or four women had been found dead in their baths people began to think there was something rather odd going on. Mind you, none of the other brides were called Smith, but inquiry showed that the groom in every case had been the same. If ever a fellow committed suicide, it was Smith. It's always a mistake to stick to a technique simply because it was successful the first time.'

She said rigidly, 'Will you tell me what all this has to do with Barbara Hurst?'

'The first time I met the young lady she was nurse-companion to a Miss Harriet Carter—this was a little over a month ago. Miss Carter was old, self-opinionated and with very few living relatives. She made a will . . . can you guess what was in it?'

'She left something to Barbara Hurst?'

'That's right. Nine thousand pounds. It was virtually all she had. Then one day something happened; she decided to change the will; I got a message to go over the next morning.' He stopped.

'It's like being in an underground train that keeps stopping for no reason,' cried the goaded girl. 'What happened when you got there?'

'I learned that she'd died the night before—in her sleep—unexpectedly—of an overdose of sleeping tablets.'

'And—I was suspected? Go on, tell me. Is that why . . .?'

'Why what?'

She doubled her hands and pressed them against her breast, in an instinctive gesture. He found it oddly moving.

'When I realised I was lost, didn't know my name, my address, why I should be at Beachampton at all, the obvious course was to go to the police. And I couldn't. Mr Menzies, I couldn't. I didn't know why, but something stopped me. And I suppose that's the answer—that I was accused of Miss Carter's murder.'

'My dear Miss Hurst, you know very well nothing of the kind happened. If you'd been accused of murder you certainly wouldn't have been free to lose your personality at Beachampton a month later.'

'Then—what did happen?'

'Must you keep up the act while we're alone?' he asked curiously.

'It's not an act. Oh, how stupid can a man be? I'm not such a fool I haven't followed you. Miss Carter's death wasn't a natural one, someone had given her an overdose, I was in charge—did I handle the medicines?—therefore I did it. I must have been a fool, because surely it would be obvious who was responsible. What do they call the Policeman's Unholy Trinity? Means, motive and opportunity. I can see I should have had means and opportunity—what about motive?'

'She'd sent for me.'

'To alter her will?'

'What other reason could an old lady have for summoning her lawyer?'

'You assume she was going to cut me out. Did anyone ever say so?'

'You were virtually the only legatee. She couldn't improve your position, and if she proposed to improve anyone else's it could only be at your expense. I don't say no one else could have been involved, but it was to everyone else's interest that she should live long enough to change the will.'

68

All this time Barbara had been listening rather like someone in a daze; now it came to her that this person they were discussing so coolly, who had handed an old woman a poisoned medicine glass and then waited for the results, was herself. And suddenly she laughed. No one was more amazed than she; she hastened to explain.

'It's not funny, of course it's not funny. Just fantastic. To think that I would want anything so much that I'd commit a murder—because that's what you're really saying, isn't it? You're saying I poisoned her, because perhaps she was going to revoke her will. Doesn't anyone know, by the way, why she wanted to see a lawyer?'

'It was thought at the inquest that Barbara Hurst might know.'

'And she wouldn't tell?'

'She said she had only learned by chance that I'd been summoned.'

'So—what happened?'

'The coroner's jury decided there wasn't enough positive evidence to support a verdict of murder against any particular person, and the funeral took place a day or two later.'

'Was I there?' She felt the strong tide of hysteria rising within her. 'Not that it matters what you tell me. I'm bound to believe you because I've no knowledge of my own to refute anything you say. And did it take place at Beachampton? Is that why I was there?'

He said sharply, 'Keep calm. You won't help anyone by having hysterics. No, you weren't at the funeral, and when the household reassembled you'd gone—presumably to Beachampton.'

'Not even leaving an address?'

'Not even leaving an address.'

'I must have gone out of my mind. Didn't you say I was an heiress? It wouldn't make much sense me poisoning Miss Carter if I didn't hang around to collect, as they say.'

'You wouldn't expect to have an estate cleared up in a month, though, would you? And you haven't any relatives or any private means. You had a job in a hat shop that went bankrupt

69

before you came to Miss Carter. So it would mean going out on the old trail—now do you begin to understand why I mentioned George Joseph Smith?'

She had been pale before, but now the blood seemed to flow downwards from her face till its whiteness alarmed him.

'The mixture as before,' she said at last.

He crossed the room quickly, catching her by the upper arm. 'In a sense you might say I'm acting for you. Go upstairs and pack your things. Send yourself a telegram calling yourself back to London or Timbuktu or Tibet, it doesn't matter where, but— *get out of this house.*'

She shook her head. 'You don't understand. I can't leave Mrs Calmady now. I'm not deceiving her any more, she knows I'm not Barbara Fitton.'

'Have I your permission to tell her you're Barbara Hurst?'

'Oh no, no!' The denial poured from her lips. 'She must never know. You understand—never. She trusts me.'

His face, that had been softening, closed up again. 'Miss Carter trusted you, Miss Hurst. And she died.'

She cried breathlessly, 'You're a lawyer, you must know you can't make unfounded charges. . . .'

'I'm making no charges. Merely pointing out facts. Will you do as I suggest? Will you pack your things and by hook or crook be ready to leave this house with me this afternoon?'

'Of course not,' she panted. 'It would be an admission that I knew something about Miss Carter's death.'

'Your own claim is that you know nothing. If everything had been above-board would you have lost your memory so conveniently? It's a case of Nature throwing up a barrier to camouflage something you'd prefer to forget.'

'Then it's odd it should happen to me and not to other people—your Mr Smith, for instance. But no, I will not be bulldozed. This is my job, I've undertaken to stay and so long as they're satisfied with me, here I shall remain. And, if any harm comes to Mrs Calmady, you may be sure I shan't be responsible.'

He put up a hand and pushed back his hair. 'All right,' he

said. 'But I'm the Calmadys' lawyer, too. I must tell them the facts.'

'Not Mrs Calmady. You don't understand. She can't take shocks. And she's already had one during the past 24 hours.'

'All right,' he said, 'I'll tell Calmady and shift the responsibility on to him. And I still don't think it would be a bad idea for you to pack that bag.'

The door opened briskly and Julie came in. She looked very pale and unnaturally composed.

'Why, Barbara, I didn't realise you were back yet,' she said. 'Mother has been asking for you. You'd better go up now.'

Something in the girl's manner struck her as strange; coming closer, she caught her by the arm.

'What's the matter with you? Are you feeling ill?' Her inquisitive gaze went from the girl's white face to Menzies' impassive one. 'What's going on here?'

Barbara wrenched her arm away. 'Ask Mr Menzies. I'm going up.'

'You'd better not go into Mother looking like that, unless you want her to have a heart attack on the spot; she'll think you're a ghost.' She turned back to the lawyer. 'You're staying to lunch, of course?'

'Your mother kindly suggested it.'

'Then that's settled. What are you waiting for, Barbara? Hadn't you better finish the hand? You've played your cards so well it would be a pity to throw away the rubber now, before the codicil's signed.'

Menzies looked as though he would speak but thought better of it; Barbara sent him an imploring glance, but he made no response. She turned with a desperate movement and left the room.

'What has happened?' demanded Julie, as the door closed behind her. 'That girl looked as if she would drop where she stood. Had you told her Mother wasn't leaving her anything, after all?'

'Will you get hold of your cousin?' Menzies inquired. 'Now. There's something I think you should both know.'

'About Barbara?' Her eyes brightened.

71

'Yes.'

'You mean, you know something about her?'

'I mean, Mrs Calmady's my client. I can't risk distressing her, so I think I should confide what I know—not, I should stress, drawing any particular conclusions, just reciting the facts—in her daughter and nephew.'

Julie's eyes were blazing. She ran to the door. 'Miles! Miles.'

He came out of the library looking rather troubled. 'What is it, Julie? Not your mother?'

'It's Mr Menzies. He can tell us something about your precious Barbara.'

Menzies looked up as Miles came in. 'I've just warned Miss Hurst that I'm going to tell you this, and you must use your own judgment about passing it on to Mrs Calmady.'

'Miss Hurst?'

'That is Miss Field's real name.'

Julie clashed her hands together. 'I knew she was a phony, a charlatan. I told Mother so. What happened to make her change her name—if Hurst really is hers? She seems to change it pretty easily. Are the police after her?'

'No,' said Menzies. 'But she's just passed through a very distressing ordeal.'

It was odd, thought Menzies, how Julie's gloating dislike of the girl aroused in him something approaching a feeling of championship. It was absurd, contrary to all his knowledge of her, for hadn't he been at the inquest, and couldn't he swear that, short of actual evidence, it had been her hand that gave the poison to the unsuspecting old woman? A tough little gold-digger who didn't draw the line at murder—that was Barbara Hurst, with her engaging ways and soft voice—not the first to deceive a man. He thought of Philip Crane, the doctor to whom she'd been engaged; and then he realised his audience were expecting to be told what he was driving at.

He made the story as concise as possible, carefully apportioning no blame. But it sounded pretty black all the same; it was obvious both the Calmadys thought so.

'Of course she did it,' said Julie. 'Who else could?'

'There was the nephew, Ralph Carter, a nasty bit of work,

I thought—middle-aged man, who'd accepted a good many favours from the old lady in the past, but never bothered to come and see her until it seemed likely she wouldn't be with us much longer, and then, of course, he hustled over to secure his inheritance. It's no secret that he was furious to discover old Miss Carter had left practically every penny over which she had any power to Barbara Hurst.'

'I don't blame him,' said Julie. 'He was the relation. . . .'

'There was an income that came through Miss Carter's father that was secured to Ralph. But in addition the old lady had had a legacy from a godmother and she had her savings. She was very canny as they say in Scotland, and I hardly imagine she spent twenty-five pounds a year on personal expenses during those last few years. Anyway, there was a total of about £9000, all of which was willed to the girl, for whom Miss Carter had a great affection.'

'And how long had she been working there?' demanded Julie excitably.

'Nearly two years.'

'Why, that's at the rate of about £5000 a year. Do you mean she murdered Miss Carter?'

'I mean that Miss Carter died suddenly and an inquest was ordered. It was declared that she had taken about twice as much of a certain drug as was prescribed and it had proved fatal. She used to have two tablets every night, which were given her with some kind of milk chocolate drink, by Barbara Hurst. On the night in question Miss Hurst telephoned the doctor to say she needed a fresh supply of tablets. She didn't pretend the last phial was empty, she simply said it had disappeared.'

'And you mean to say the doctor believed a thin story like that?' Julie's voice was sick with scorn.

'It's rather a strange situation. This fellow—Crane—was engaged to Miss Hurst. The whole thing must have come as an appalling shock to him. By chance it wasn't he who had to give the certificate, he'd been called out to an emergency and the doctor who was called in wasn't satisfied.'

'And Barbara was accused of murder?'

'No, no. No such accusation has ever been made. But she had

to answer some very awkward questions at the inquest. She said the phial of tablets must have been thrown away accidentally during the afternoon. The nephew, Ralph Carter, had come down to sort papers with his aunt, and the tablets were on a bed-table—he recalls seeing them—and of course they could easily have rolled off and been thrown into a waste-paper basket.'

'Didn't Barbara think of looking in the basket?'

'All the stuff was put on the tradesman's lift and wound down by the porter to be in readiness for the dust collector the next morning. Anyway, Dr Crane sent round the tablets, and the next day two were missing. That would be a normal dose; the remainder were vetted before the inquest, and they tallied with the prescription. So it was clear that she must have had an overdose, and the question was—who gave it her?'

'There can't be two opinions about that,' cried Julie. 'Barbara did, of course. Do you mean to say she got away with it? What's become of justice in this country?'

'Was there a motive?' asked Miles.

'Of course there was. Mr Menzies has just told us she was the prospective heir, and the old lady was going to change her will, learnt something, I suppose, to open her eyes to the viper she was cherishing in her bosom; so before it was too late Barbara took action. How on earth did she manage to bamboozle the jury?'

'Presumably they didn't consider the case against her was strong enough to take into court. There were other people on the premises, remember, and so long as there's a shadow of reasonable doubt, no jury would dare convict.'

'They might consider the general public, instead of turning a girl like that loose on the world,' was Julie's fierce comment. 'Fancy taking another job in almost identical circumstances! She must be very sure of her technique.'

'Her story is that she recalls nothing of Miss Carter or her position in that household. If that is the case, her instinct would most probably lead her into the only kind of situation with which she's familiar. In a sense, the very fact of her being here supports her own story.'

Miles intervened, 'Didn't you say something about an old servant? Could she conceivably have been responsible? I understand, of course,' he added quickly, 'that no such suggestion was made at the inquest, but—in your opinion was that a possibility?'

Menzies frowned. 'It would be difficult to prove a motive for Wotton. All she inherited was a couple of rooms of indifferent furniture and £50 in cash. Not much after nearly twenty years.'

Julie's eyes looked as though they would pop out of her head. 'Do you mean to say that's all she got after all that time, while Barbara was to get £9000 for less than two years?'

'Miss Carter belonged to the old school. When she was a daughter of the Manse the village girls queued up to enter service at the big house; it was a privilege. When Wotton came to her I dare say she had the same idea of providing a pension in due course that the family had always had, but then we got the Welfare State. Free doctoring, free dentistry, retirement pension, National Assistance Board—it didn't seem to the old lady that private people should be expected to make provision any more. She had to pay the full stamp each week—Wotton didn't pay anything, of course, being past contributory age—and according to Miss Carter (she explained all this to me with the most pedantic thoroughness) she must have saved the greater part of her wages all this time. And then there was the sister, who was a widow living in the country, with a couple of empty rooms that would just suit Wotton in due course.'

Miles asked curiously, 'Did it occur to her that after about thirty years, the two old ladies mightn't hit it off?'

'I told you, Miss Carter belonged to the old school. Families stick together, they have duties, blood's thicker than water and so forth. Oh, she thought she had made ample provision. The fifty pounds was to cover the cost of shifting the furniture to Mrs Marsh's house—that's the sister—and what was left over would buy Wotton a mourning get-up. No, I can't see any reason why Wotton should want to risk her neck putting the old lady out of the way. And in any case she hadn't the opportunity, since Miss Carter had had her nightcap, plus the pills, by the time Wotton returned. The only possible thing she could have done was put the missing tablets into the milk that she left poured out in the larder; it's just barely possible that she did it, in the sense that she could have picked up the phial and abstracted a number of tablets, but it's not an argument that would carry any weight, because Ralph Carter says the tablets were on the bed-table when he arrived that afternoon.'

'And no one else came in?' Julie's face was red with excitement. 'Then of course Barbara did it; and Mother shall be told before she signs that codicil.'

She looked as if she would rush away on the instant, but for Miles's detaining hand.

'Be careful, Julie. Your mother's already had one severe shock in the last 24 hours. Her heart can't stand much more strain.'

'I'm afraid, Miss Calmady, I haven't made the situation clear,' said Menzies. 'The codicil has been signed, and witnessed by the woman who works here, and a Mrs Luke who, I understand, helps with the washing. The whole thing's sewn up, as they say.'

Julie stared as if she couldn't believe her ears. 'And you let that girl go up to Mother? Who are you acting for? Her? Or us?'

Menzies did his best to compose her. 'Miss Hurst knows nothing of the execution of the codicil,' he urged. 'I purposely didn't tell her.'

'*You* didn't tell her! But what about my mother? You can be sure Barbara will rush straight in and find out how the land lies, and once she knows the money's safe . . .'

'Oh, don't talk nonsense, Julie,' Miles interposed. 'The girl's not a howling idiot. She knows Menzies has just told us this story about Miss Carter. Do you imagine she's going to fly straight upstairs and make herself liable to suspicion of murder for the second time in six weeks?'

'Well, I'm going up at once,' Julie announced, and at that instant the bell from Mrs Calmady's room rang with a shrill insistence that brought all three of them running.

In the old woman's room Barbara was bowed beside the bed.

One arm was about the frail shoulders, the hand of the other
had been frantically pressing the bell. Indeed, she went on
ringing even after their appearance till Miles stopped her.

'What's going on?' Julie demanded.

'Get Dr Stuart quickly. It's the drops, her drops. She must
have tried to take them when she was alone, because they've
spilled over the bed. I couldn't even find the tube at first, then
I saw it had rolled under the bed. Oh, call the doctor quickly,
though even at that he'll be too late.'

Miles said over his shoulder, 'Menzies, would you get him?
Seven-two. Tell him it's urgent.'

He settled on the other side of the bed, lifted one flaccid
eyelid. 'Julie, the brandy!'

But when she had opened a cupboard and produced it, it was
no good. The colourless lips could not contain the liquid, which
dribbled over the sheet.

'What did you say to her to put her in this state?'

Menzies came back from the telephone just in time to hear
the question.

'I didn't say anything,' returned Barbara dully. 'She wouldn't
have been capable of understanding if I had. I'll never forgive
myself for this all my life.'

'Take care!' The warning sprang instinctively to Menzies's
lips.

Miles said, 'What does that mean, Barbara?'

'Julie told me that she was asking for me and I should have
come straight in. But I'd had rather a shock—no doubt Mr
Menzies himself has told you—and Julie said I looked like
someone who'd crawled out of a grave or words to that
effect—so I didn't come straight in. I went along to wash and
put on a little colour. I was five minutes perhaps. If I hadn't
wasted that time I might have got here before she tried to take
the drops herself. But what I don't understand is why she didn't
ring. She always rang—except, of course, she didn't know I
was back.'

Even Menzies, the experienced man, shuddered at the look
these simple words brought to Julie's face.

'I have been known to give Mother her drops,' she returned

77

thickly. 'And while we're on the subject of the bell, I should think it would be obvious to everyone why she didn't ring it—*why you didn't mean her to.*'

They all looked instinctively towards the bell. My mythical Belinda, old Mrs Calmady used to say. It was Menzies who spoke first.

'Could she have reached it in its present position?' he inquired. 'It was a good deal closer to her when she showed it me an hour ago.'

'It was a good deal closer when I left her not a quarter of an hour ago,' put in Julie. 'It was always put well within reach.'

'Then I suppose I pushed it out of the way while I was looking for the tablets,' said Barbara in a confused voice. 'I hadn't noticed it had been shifted, but, of course, you're right.'

She looked down at old Mrs Calmady; already the face was settling into the anonymity of death; breath came so slow and shallow between the pale lips it was scarcely perceptible. Soon, before Dr Stuart's car came racing up the drive, it had ceased altogether. Miles laid his head against the thin bosom. Then he took the old hands and folded them tenderly.

'It's no good. Barbara, don't blame yourself. It's just one of those things. She must have felt the attack coming on and groped for the drops. . . .'

'Why didn't she ring the bell?'

'She may have thought she could manage. I suppose the battery hasn't given way? No, of course not. Barbara summoned us by it. Well, I suppose faintness overcame her.'

'She was perfectly calm when I left her and when I came down to find Barbara. I can't think of a single reason why she should suddenly have an attack while she was by herself. And if you're going to tell me it's sheer concidence that two old women should die very conveniently with Miss Barbara Hurst in attendance, then all I can say is I hope this time the coroner's jury shows a little more sense. It certainly won't be my fault if they don't know the facts.'

'Be careful, Julie, there's such a thing as a law of slander. You've no proof whatever of what you've just said, and Barbara had no idea the codicil that left her a bequest had been signed and witnessed.'

'What's that?' Barbara looked up sharply. 'Who says so?'

'Mr Menzies has just told us.'

'And my mother had just told you. Of course she had. She'd be bursting to give you the good news, and you saw that you only had a minute or two before she was introduced to *Barbara Hurst*, but a minute was enough. I dare say it didn't take any longer to give Miss Carter her overdose, too.'

Barbara stood up, facing them all. 'I can't answer anything about Miss Carter, because I don't remember anything. I don't feel as though I were Barbara Hurst, because she's no more than a name to me. Mr Menzies says it's my name. Well, I take his word for it. No doubt it will be easy enough to prove. But I begin to wonder if I'm going on in the dark for the rest of my life. I always believed once I met someone from the past everything would become clear.'

'The rest of your life!' repeated Julie. 'If you go on like this there won't be much 'rest' for you to trouble about. One of these days you'll over-reach yourself—I wonder what name you'll be using then—and someone will point out that it's rather odd, isn't it, that wherever you go some helpless old person dies—and you're enriched thereby.'

The words poured out of her mouth; she was like a little ship tossed in a storm, she seemed past control, veering hither and thither. One thing, reflected Menzies, no one would hang a mouse on the evidence of a creature so clearly unbalanced as Julie Calmady.

CHAPTER 6

The arrival of Dr Stuart made a fortunate break. He came marching in, still wearing his overcoat, and the situation was explained to him. He thrust them all aside and bent over his patient, but it took no more than a few seconds for him to give his verdict. He asked the minimum of questions, heard Julie's frantic statement, Miles's calm one, and Barbara's stammering one; he agreed that matters had probably happened as the girl surmised, offered sympathy all round, assured them that the essential certificate would be readily available and went downstairs, telling Miles that it had at best been a matter of weeks, more probably of days, and added that any suffering must have been mercifully brief.

'Don't let that girl start making herself sick over this,' he added. 'This was bound to happen some time and no one could have said when.'

Julie was furious. 'I always knew he was a stupid old man,' she declared. 'Now I realise he's lazy as well. The line of least resistance for him every time. One thing I do know—Barbara Hurst leaves this house at once.'

On Menzies's advice, however, Barbara agreed to remain until after the funeral.

'You're virtually living in a village,' he told the Calmdys. 'Your affairs are everyone's affairs. If Miss Hurst leaves the house immediately after the old lady's death the whole place will start putting two and two together. It's bound to come out that she's a beneficiary under the will, and either they'll start a mutter about foul play or tell each other that the girl had to get out because of the bad blood engendered by the legacy, and believe me, your position will be unenviable in either case. Let her stay till after the funeral, and then it will seem perfectly natural for her to go back to London. And I do earnestly advise you, Miss Calmady, to reconsider your resolve to try and upset the will. As a lawyer I can assure you your only hope would be to bring a charge of murder against Miss Hurst, a charge you certainly couldn't substantiate.'

'There's such a thing as undue influence. You'll never make me believe that girl didn't come here with the express intention of lining her own nest. Yes, of course she did, Miles. She had your letter, she knew where we lived, probably she knew all about us before she came near that hotel. And now she's pulled it off for the second time. I wonder either of you can square it with your conscience to take no action.'

'Your cousin has worked herself into a dangerous state over this,' Menzies warned Miles Calmady. 'Isn't there somewhere where she can get away? Does she really grudge that girl her legacy? She herself is being left most comfortably off.'

'Oh, it's not just the money,' said Miles, sighing. 'Candidly I can't see any satisfactory future for her. And I wish I could feel more confident that things were going to work out all right for Barbara. Has she any plans, I wonder?'

'She's full of them,' Menzis assured him. 'The first shock is wearing off, and she's beginning to tell herself that as she took no active part in Mrs Calmady's death it's probable that she had nothing to do with Miss Carter's. I must admit that at the outset I thought this rigmarole about loss of memory was a clever bit of bluff. Now I'm inclined to think there may be something in it. If not, she's a first-rate actress, and it isn't natural to be on guard 24 hours of the day.'

Miles looked at him in surprise. 'I never doubted it,' he said. 'It explained so many things that had puzzled me, her indifference to her mythical father and his new wife, the fact that she never received letters or wrote them—Julie was smart enough to spot that. . . .'

'A girl who was acting the part *would* have written letters,' insisted Menzies. 'She wouldn't have posted them or she'd have posted them to fictitious addresses, but she certainly wouldn't have neglected anything so obvious.'

'And then she never spoke of the past, none of those casual references people make—Oh, I was there five years ago—or—My mother always shopped at Bourne and Hollingsworth—never a personal note of any kind . . . Menzies, what must it be like to be walking in the dark on a razor edge? And suppose she never gets back?'

'Maybe when she does she may wish she hadn't,' was the lawyer's cryptic reply. 'Don't make any mistake about it—it was some shock of a considerable order that brought on this condition, and although she believes a meeting with some of the people who made up that old life will effect a cure, personally I'm less optimistic. So far nothing's rung a bell. Did you happen to mention my name, before I turned up?'

'Yes. I said you were coming in place of Cutbush.'

'And she never turned a hair. The names meant nothing to her. A girl who was play-acting would have seen the red light. I fancy she's banking her hopes on Crane.'

'The chap who was going to marry her? I don't think he's much use—a real broken reed. He might at least have kept his eye on her, instead of which he appears to have broken the engagement. . . .'

'I fancy that was her doing. He came back from the funeral or after the funeral and the girl had gone, sunk without trace. Did it occur to you she'd taken special pains not to go off with anything that could identify her? I wonder what a psychologist would make of that.'

'That she wanted to forget,' agreed Miles sensibly. 'But— what? That she was guilty? That Crane thought her guilty?'

'He says he told he he'd stand by her, no matter what the suspicion, that she seemed comparatively calm, wouldn't come to the funeral because Wotton—that's the housekeeper—and Carter and his wife made it clear they thought she was responsible—and then—I suppose she'd been laying this plan for some days. Crane came to see me, wanted to know what he could do. Well, I said, you can put a private dick on to her if you like, but I don't recommend it. The girl's free, white and twenty-one, and she's got your address. I will say for him he was very much upset, but whether that was because he thought she'd done it or because he was afraid she might have put herself in the river, I wouldn't like to guess.'

'And now?' demanded Miles. 'In a sense she's going to be worse off than she was with us.'

'She's my client in a sense. I've told her as much. That gives me a handle. I'll keep an eye on her, and she's full of a plan to go round seeing everyone until she's unearthed the truth. I only hope she'll have the sense to keep it to herself if it's not what she anticipates.'

The period between the death and the burial seemed interminable. In the household friction was only avoided by Julie taking to her room and refusing to leave it. Florrie brought up her meals, divided between a sense of respect for filial grief and indignation at the extra work put upon her. Miles and Barbara took their meals together, but avoided one another as much as possible for the rest of the day. The funeral itself took place in wet weather, and the mourners stood under umbrellas on a concrete path while a shuddering clergyman committed the body to the earth as rapidly as decency would permit. There were flowers from many who could hardly have been expected to pay such a tribute to the dead, but Barbara realised that there had been a fund of secret charity about the dead woman that even Julie had not suspected. The party returned to the house, the blinds, that had been drawn down after the Edwardian fancy, were raised, Florrie produced a meal, Menzies read the will unemotionally, and left for London almost immediately afterwards. He offered Barbara a place in the car he was hiring to take him back to town, which she was grateful to accept. For most of the journey they preserved silence; only as they reached the outskirts of the Green Belt, Menzies roused himself to say, 'Have you any plan in mind, as to where you'll go to-night, for instance?'

She said vaguely, 'A hotel, I suppose,' to which he replied, 'You've certainly forgotten what London's like. It's not easy to get in anywhere just now. Remember, I represent you, unless you refuse my services and frankly I doubt if you'd be wise.

Yours is such a very remarkable story, so, speaking as your lawyer, naturally I'm bound to believe in your good faith until the reverse has been proved.'

'I suppose nothing will convince you that I'm telling the truth.'

He replied diplomatically, 'Shall we say that I'd like to afford you every opportunity to prove that you are?'

After this he became unexpectedly helpful and kind. It appeared that he had a client who had gone abroad at very short notice, leaving her furnished flat in his hands.

'She'll be away for several weeks and she's asked us to find a responsible tenant. She's asking rather stiff terms, but it's a convenient flat, and she's expressed a preference for a woman, because she thinks they're more careful as a rule about things like cigarette burns. I didn't disillusion her by telling her that I've known women who'd put a hot saucepan on the top of the grand piano, I simply told her I'd make sure our candidate wouldn't abscond without paying the rent, and would respect her belongings.'

'So you are prepared to trust me to that extent? Isn't that some advance?'

'I'll show my hand thus far—I want to keep you under my eye, I'd really be glad to find you didn't have a hand in Miss Carter's death, and by that I mean I should be genuinely pleased to find some proof that your story is true. A couple of centuries ago, Barbara Hurst, you'd have been burnt for a witch. From the facts, in so far as I know them, I've no reason at all to credit your *bona fides*, but I want them to be true—do you get that? There's no doubt at all that Miles Calmady believes you. And you certainly laid a spell on both the old ladies. As for the rent part of it, I can take that into my own hands, by stopping the payments out of your legacy. Oh, I know you haven't got it yet, but Miss Carter's will was the least complicated I've ever come across. It shouldn't take long to wind up. She believed in supporting the country's war effort and she didn't follow the example of a great many people and sell out her securities as soon as V-J Day was announced. It's unfortunate that gilt-edged isn't standing up very well to post-war economics; but she had quite a healthy amount in a Building Society and more in tin, so one way and another you should do pretty well. And, of course, the firm will lend you money against the estate until it's been settled up.'

'Where does Wotton live now?' asked Barbara.

'With her widowed sister in Hertfordshire.'

'Could I go and see her or does she hate me, too?'

'Now, come, Miss Hurst,' he adjured her, 'you can't expect too much of human nature. You walked into Miss Carter's house and Miss Carter's life like Julius Cæsar. *Veni, vidi, vici.* And at the end of it all you carry off the bulk of the spoils and Miss Wotton is, let's face it, pretty shabbily treated. You can't expect her not to feel some resentment. Quite apart from the fact,' he added coolly, 'that this must be easily the most exciting thing that's ever happened to her. As good as a film.'

'That's horrible,' cried Barbara.

'Human,' he said.

'But so unfair.'

'Life is unfair. The world's full of people who've had a raw deal. Perfectly virtuous and normal women give birth to handicapped children, innocent folk are struck down by polio, or lose those they love best in senseless accidents. What I'm driving at is that if, as I'm bound to hope, your memory is restored and you know yourself to be innocent, don't let it cloud your life that you can't prove it. Life's never been fair and injustice strikes wherever it will, like the rain falling on the just and the unjust. Accept the past and put it behind you.'

Arthur Crook wouldn't have agreed with him, of course. No one was going to do Arthur Crook injustice and get away with it; but at that stage Barbara had never heard the indomitable lawyer's name.

Arrived in London he took her to see the flat, which was small, but commodious and centrally situated. Later he brought her the box of personal belongings that had been stored in the room behind the office where the clients' deed-boxes were housed, and she spent some time unpacking her possessions. Menzies had supplied the addresses both of Crane and of

Wotton, but it appeared that the doctor had been called away on a consultation and was not expected back until late that evening.

'You've got all the time there is,' Menzies told her. 'Let me know how it goes, and if there's anything we can do to help you can count on us. And I should like your promise not to take any form of employment without consulting me first.'

'You're being very kind,' murmured Barbara in a confused voice.

'Am I? The fact is, your enthusiasm for discovering the past is rather disarming. It makes you sound so young. If anyone had told me three days ago that I should hope so urgently you weren't responsible for what happened in Miss Carter's flat, I'd have thought him crazy.'

As he was going, she said, her face suddenly clouding over and the youthfulness he had just praised being blotted out like the features of a landscape as a sudden storm gathers, 'Suppose in spite of everything I find I can't prove my innocence? Do you imagine it's going to help me to realise that other people have had a raw deal, too? What about the future? Could I marry, have children, never being certain what kind of legacy I was handing on to them?'

'At the moment,' he told her bluntly, 'you're neither fish, fowl nor good red herring. You're not Barbara Field, because she never existed, but you're not Barbara Hurst either, because she's a stranger to you. Something has happened to blot out your memory, and it's pretty safe to assume that it's something you'd prefer not to recall. You're taking a chance trying to roll away the stone.'

'I dare say,' agreed Barbara briskly, 'but you can't spend your life behind a stone. I've got to know the truth, and if anybody concerned with the affair can help me I shall be like the man in the Bible who said he would take no rest and give God no rest till he had established the kingdom, the kingdom in my case being the truth.'

There was an odd compassion in the glance he turned on her. 'You don't think there may be wisdom in the old saying about letting sleeping dogs lie?'

'I do not. If they were dead dogs perhaps—but sleeping dogs must waken sometime. By the way, what do I call Dr Crane?'

'That's an odd question,' he exclaimed. 'Philip, of course. That's his name.'

'Odd. It doesn't seem to rouse any echoes. Still, I'm counting on him to be the key that will open the door back to reality. If he fails me, then I'm lost indeed.'

He left the flat, taking with him an impression of youth and a sincerity it was hard to deny, though he reminded himself sternly that it's never safe to judge by appearances. When he had gone, Barbara set about unpacking her belongings and bestowing them in the appropriate cupboards and drawers. When this was done she glanced at her watch and saw with amazement it was no more than six o'clock. Everything had happened with such expedition that between the funeral, that had taken place at noon, and the present moment there had been ample time to hear the will, make her arrangements, travel to town, settle herself in this temporary home, and still the long evening stretched before her, as empty as a desert. A small portable wireless had been among her possessions and she switched this on to listen to the news, but there was nothing of import, and soon she turned it off again. She went out and had a meal at a nearby café, a modern bare clean place with patterned walls and bright scarlet tables and chairs. Not many people were there at this hour, the waiting was quick and by seven o'clock she was back again in the street. What to do now? A cinema? But the first house she came to was showing an American shocker, and the next a French film dealing with savagery in French prisons. On a sudden impulse she crossed the street to enter a telephone booth. She had dialled a number before she realised she had had no need to consult the directory. So it appeared that in spots her memory still functioned.

She heard a click as the telephone was unshipped at the other end and a voice said, 'Dr Crane speaking.' With a stealthy movement she hung up, left the box and hurried towards the nearest Underground station. Philip Crane was back, and before she went to bed that night she would test her belief that a meeting with him would release the flood-tide of memory and give her back hope and the future.

At the station they told her where she should change for Ferriby Park, and she hurried down the steps to await her train. The journey seemed interminable, yet, in a sense, she wished time could be halted and this train go on for ever. So much depended on the next hour or so. She realised she did not know Crane's address and when she arrived she looked for it in a telephone directory, before mounting to the street. Now fever rose in her like milk boiling up in a saucepan. Now, surely, when she found herself in familiar surroundings, memory would raise its head, she would know the way—but nothing of the sort happened. She found with shock that she could not even supply Miss Carter's address. Standing on the pavement outside the station, staring over the tree-bordered common that separated her from the residential quarter, she knew she was as lost as if she were in a desert. St Gilda's Terrace was her destination, 27 the number of the house. For the first time it occurred to her that Dr Crane might have a visitor, or more than one; or he might be summoned out on a sick call, but she had come too far to turn back now. The station supplied no local map for her guidance and there seemed a dearth of passers-by. A succession of scarlet buses went past, and she knew she had only to question one of the conductors to be put on her way, but each time she hesitated just too long and saw the great red monster go roaring down to the High Street. Eventually a policeman, seeing her dismay, crossed the street to know if he could be of help. Her involuntary start at the sight of him was not lost upon him, and he found himself wondering if she were in some sort of trouble; to his eye she had an unprotected air, and he hoped she contemplated no rash action.

'It seems absurd,' she acknowledged, 'I lived here at one time, but it's a little while ago and I seem to have lost my bearings. I want St Gilda's Terrace, but everything looks so different in the dark.'

For by now the evening had come down and away from the lamps the world was dim with shadow. He told her to cross the common and turn right up the hill. It was quicker to walk than to take a bus, since St Gilda's Terrace was a residential street and no public transport ran along it. She did look round vaguely for a taxi, but the rank was empty now, so, with a word of thanks, she set forth on her journey.

The common was quite countrified so late in the evening, and pretty soon she was clear of the range of the lamps set like saplings along its borders, Sundry whispers and movements in the darkness warned her that it was a resort of lovers, and she put down her head and hurried along the narrow path. She was in a nervous state and no mistake, she told herself, for while she went, careful to avoid the trails of bramble that obstructed her way, she was haunted by a story she had once read—a novel? A case in a newspaper? She couldn't be sure—of another girl who, in like predicament, had been crossing an open space and suddenly heard steps coming up behind her and, before she could turn, had felt the ends of the long scarf she wore caught and drawn close about her throat, and had died there in the darkness, unable even to utter a cry.

'I am certainly taking leave of my senses,' she told herself angrily, 'this is a suburb of London, there are people all about me, a policeman not five minutes away, and for all I know there's a second one on the other side of the common. It won't help me to discover who I am if that self proves to be a lunatic.'

Nevertheless, she could not dispel that inward fear that caused her breath to come short and sharp between her lips and her body to tremble as if oppressed with cold. The wind pattering up behind her rustled some leaves and she swerved wildly, entangling herself in a bush whose existence she had overlooked in her haste. She felt a stocking ladder, stooped to tear it free and then almost ran to the farther side of the common. Even the clumps of bushes took on the semblance of crouched human figures awaiting her approach, and once in making a detour she all but tripped over a couple lying sprawled on the dry ground. It was a clear cool night with a dark velvet sky pricked with stars that gave little light; and there was no moon. At length she emerged, panting and dishevelled, and paused at the corner of a quiet street to effect some repairs. To arrive at the doctor's house looking as though she had just escaped from a bear-pit would be no recommendation for a reasonable hearing. She kept reminding herself that this stranger whom she was hurrying to meet was the man to whom she had once engaged herself, for whom she had presumably experienced passionate feeling. Yet, though she repeated his name over and over, it aroused no echo in her heart.

'But when I see him I shall know, I am certain that I shall know,' she reassured herself.

The house was tall and narrow, with a brass plate inscribed Dr Philip Crane and his qualifications. A light burned in an upper window, and she took heart from this, since surely it proved he hadn't gone out since her call. Pushing open the gate she ran up the path and rang the bell.

CHAPTER 7

Philip Crane was listening to a radio programme when he heard the sound of the front-door bell. He frowned. This was his free evening of the week, when, by arrangement with a panel of local doctors, his surgery patients attended one of his colleagues. That mysterious telephone call annoyed him; he didn't think it was someone trying to find out if the house was occupied, with any thought of breaking and entering in mind. It wouldn't pay the least ambitious housebreaker to raid No 27. No, it was one of his neurotic patients—every doctor has a few—imagining herself no end cunning and ringing up to find out if he was on the premises. Well, he told himself irritably, she could go on ringing till she got tired. And if it was anyone else, he was in no mood for visitors.

After the bell had rung for the third time, however, his patience broke; he turned down the radio and went pelting down the stairs. It wasn't an accident summons, he knew that before he opened the door. *That* bell would have been urgent, imperious, and the chap ringing it would never have taken his finger off the button. This ring had a timid sound—someone who had no right to be there, he concluded grimly.

He opened the door prepared to say it was a mistake, before he saw who it was, and then the words dried on his lips and his heart seemed to fall through his body.

'Barbara!' His hand caught her arm.

She came over the step into the lighted hall, her blue eyes staring desperately into his.

'You're Dr Crane? Philip?' she implored.

He looked astounded. 'Well, of course, Barbara, pull yourself together. What on earth . . . ?'

She heard the tremble of despair in her voice as she cried back to him, 'But I don't know you, I don't know you. So far as I can tell I never even saw you before. Oh, what am I going to do now?'

His arm about her shoulders he guided her upstairs; the little sitting-room was warm and welcoming, the radio babbled along as happily as a stream or a sunny child. He put her into a chair, said in authoritative tones, 'Don't talk till I give you the word; and in the meantime, drink this.'

She took the glass obediently, swallowed the contents and then began to look about her.

'Did I ever see this room before?'

'No, I shouldn't think so,' he agreed consideringly. 'Doctors have to be models of discretion, particularly before they're married. Barbara, where on earth have you been hiding all this while?'

'I haven't been hiding exactly. I've been at Beachampton.'

'You never even sent me a postcard.'

'How could I? I didn't even know you existed; I didn't even know there was any such person as Barbara Hurst.'

'What's that? Good Heavens, so that's the explanation. The one that never occurred to me. But—when did it happen? Why? Do you remember anything at all?'

'I hoped you could help me—as to why it happened, I mean. Mr Menzies—you remember him?'

'Of course. Where does he come into this?'

'He's the Calmadys' lawyer. The Calmadys are the people I've been working for this last month.'

'How on earth could you work for anyone if you didn't know who you are?'

'It's a very odd story. I made up a name and they wanted someone in a hurry and didn't bother over references. . . .'

'Rather a peculiar household, wasn't it?'

'Oh very. But it happened to suit me at the time.'

'And you've given up the job now?'

'You might say it's given me up.'

92

'What happened? Or was it only a temporary job, anyway?'

'It would have come to an end in any case, but, of course, the arrival of Mr Menzies, who recognised me, though, as far as I knew, I'd never set eyes on him before—well, that created the present situation. He told me about you. I hadn't any idea— I didn't even know your first name. We were engaged, weren't we?'

'You know we were.'

She shook her head. 'I only know because Mr Menzies said so, and now you confirm it. Oh, Philip, you're a doctor, can't you help me?'

'To do what? To get back?'

'What else?'

'Are you sure you want to? Nature often knows her stuff better than we do.'

She was watching him with a perplexed glance, this man she must once have loved, who, as Barbara Hurst, she presumably loved still, yet who now was more of a stranger than Miles Calmady or even the young lawyer, Robert Menzies.

'What happens to people when they get lost?' she cried. 'They must be somewhere. What's the good of asking me if I really want to discover Barbara Hurst? Don't you see, I've got to discover her? Otherwise she may leap out at me like a bogy at any time, she'd hang over my head like the Sword of Damocles. And furthermore,' she continued breathlessly, 'why should you think I don't want to meet her again? What's so sinister about her?'

He got up to refill their glasses. 'Just tell me this,' he said, with his back to her. 'This job you've been doing—what kind of a job was it?'

'I was acting as stand-in for a girl called Barbara Fitton; she was killed in an accident, and they wanted someone to take her place just for a short time.'

'You mean, pretend to be Barbara Fitton?'

'Yes. Well, I didn't know who I was. I could just as easily be Barbara Fitton as anyone else.' She saw his face as he turned with the two glasses. 'I believe you're shocked, but there was no harm in it. And anyway we told the old lady the truth in the end, and it didn't upset her. I don't care what anyone says,' she added passionately, 'it wasn't that that hastened her death.'

Philip Crane put the two glasses down on the table. 'You mean, Mrs Calmady's death?'

'Yes. Oh, we knew from the start it was a matter of days. That's why she wasn't allowed to know about her grand-daughter's death.'

He had put the drinks on the table. Now he came to sit beside her, taking her hands in his.

'Barbara, there's something I must ask you. Remember, we were in love for several months and I, at least, haven't changed. When you come back to yourself, I hope you'll find you haven't changed either. I wanted to make you my wife as soon as you were free, and I still want it. Tell me this. Do you profit in any way whatsoever by Mrs Calmady's death?'

'She's left me a legacy. That's why Mr Menzies came down.'

'And that's all tied up? I mean, she actually changed the will?'

'She added a codicil, and it was signed and witnessed, though I didn't know that till later. I was out that morning and so was Julie—that was Mrs Calmady's daughter, who's trying to make out it's my fault—but there were two women working in the house who acted as witnesses.'

'And how long afterwards . . .?' He looked at her beseech-ingly, as if he couldn't finish the sentence.

'How long after did she die, do you mean? Philip, that's what was so awful. She died the same day, died alone with all of us in the house, that's what I can't forget. I hadn't gone in because I'd only just heard who I was, and Julie and Miles—that was Julie's cousin—thought I was with her, and she was fighting for her breath and nobody came, and she tried to take the drops herself. . . . Oh, Philip, I think that picture of her dying alone will haunt me till the day of my own death.'

He took one hand away, while holding her closely with the other, and picked up one of the glasses.

'Drink this,' he said. 'You're going to need it. Was there an inquest?'

'The doctor said it wasn't necessary. It could have happened just as I said.'

'Could?'

'It did. That is, she was almost done for when I went in, and all the drops were spilled. No one could have saved her, Philip, no one, whatever Julie may say. Julie hated me from the start, and in a sense I can understand it. But she's no right to say I murdered her mother. It's not true, Philip, it's not true. I wouldn't do that to an old woman who trusted me.'

She put out a blind hand, groping for the glass.

When she had half-emptied it she had recovered sufficient spirit to say, 'And I didn't do Miss Carter any harm, did I? No matter what the appearances were it was nothing to do with me. Say it was nothing to do with me, Philip.'

She felt his arm loosen about her, then he stood up and moved away.

'I told you you were going to need that drink. Barbara, I wasn't in the house when Miss Carter died, and I wasn't there when they found the body—I gave all the evidence at the inquest—but afterwards, when a more or less open verdict had been declared, you came to me on the verge of collapse and . . .'

Barbara sprang up, her hand to her throat. 'No,' she cried defiantly, 'no, I couldn't have said it was anything to do with me.'

'You said you were responsible, but you'd had no choice. Those were your actual words and thank God they weren't spoken till after the inquest. You were responsible, but you had no choice.'

The fire came up like a great screen of flame, blinding her, so that she threw her hands over her eyes, and when she took them away again the room was black. She put out a hand and another hand held it, but she couldn't see the owner of the hand. She thought she spoke, but she couldn't have done, because no one answered; with her free hand she groped for something to hold on to, a rope or a spar, because it was like drowning in an icy sea. Nothing was real and yet this time it wasn't a dream. The darkness and the silence went on till a new fear gripped her, the fear that she had lost the power of speech as well as memory. In a voice like a rusty machine she croaked one word.

'Why?'

'Why did you do it? Or why did you tell me? I can answer the second. You were in a state of utter nervous collapse and no wonder. The coroner's jury was out a considerable time; it was bad for everyone, but worst of all for you, *because you knew the truth.* I'd had to give evidence, and that was bad enough, but consider how much more appalling it was for you. And then the verdict was brought in, you weren't named, your luck, if you can call it that, had held. I saw you afterwards, and you clung to me like—like a barnacle on a rock. 'It's all right,' you said. 'Oh, Philip, I've been so afraid they'd find out, but it's all right.' At first I thought you were feverish, I couldn't believe you meant what it seemed you meant. . . .'

'But ultimately you believed me?'

'You gave me no choice. Oh, it was lucky no one else heard you. You had enemies enough in that household.'

'You mean the housekeeper?'

'And Ralph Carter. No one could see why you should inherit after so short a term of service.'

'But why did I do it, Philip? If I told you so much I must have told you that.'

'Something had happened, Miss Carter was going to disinherit you. She'd sent for Menzies.'

'And I knew?'

'You found out.'

'And I knew why?'

He remained silent.

'It doesn't hang together,' she said slowly. 'I wouldn't want money badly enough to do a thing like that. I'm not even very jealous, not of other people's possessions. I like lovely things, of course—who doesn't?—but I'd never lie awake worrying because I hadn't got them. No, you must be wrong. There must have been some other reason.'

'What reason?' His voice was gentle, but implacable as stone. 'Believe me, Barbara, I've been over and over this. Oh, it's clear something happened that last day: if I'd known about the nephew coming I'd have wired him to wait twenty-four hours; she was disturbed about something. Like a fool, I thought it was this chap, Carter, knowing there was precious little love lost between them.'

She said again, 'The reason, Philip, the reason.'

'There's only one possibility—she was going to change her will.'

'How much difference would that make to us?'

'Well, it would have made a considerable difference,' he had to acknowledge. 'I had the chance of a country practice—we both wanted to be in the country—and I hadn't the necessary capital. Miss Carter knew of our plans and appeared to approve them. Then came this—body-blow.'

'You mean, we couldn't have got married?'

'Well, not immediately. But—we were both young enough to wait, and there'd have been other chances. I tried to say that to you, but you said she had no right to raise our hopes and then dash them for a whim—a whim, you said.'

'It was her money,' Barbara murmured, and he threw back his head sharply to exclaim: 'So you do remember something, if it's only a word here and there. That's what I said to you when you told me.'

'But from all I've heard of her, she wouldn't do a thing like that out of malice. She must have had some reason. Didn't I tell you what it was when I told you everything else?'

'I don't know if you knew. Remember, it was only by chance that you had heard of Menzies's visit. And that evening you were alone in the house with Miss Carter. Ralph had gone and old Wotton was out at the Sisterhood. You rang me to ask for a fresh supply of tablets, and I sent 'em round, though I told you she ought to have some left. You said the phial was missing, it might have got thrown away, anyway she must have them, and if the old ones turned up it wouldn't matter, they could be used later.'

'And the suggestion is that they weren't missing at all, but I'd made up my mind to give her an overdose and wanted to be covered at every step?'

97

Dr Crane nodded.

'You saw me then. Did I give you the impression I was mad?'

'I'll tell you what did shock me—that you didn't seem able to take in the seriousness of what had happened. She had only a few days anyhow, you said. Don't let's think about her any more.'

'I'm beginning to see why I lost my identity,' Barbara conceded. 'Tell me—was I very much in love?'

He said quietly, 'I thought so. And so did Miss Carter. She said to me once, "You're very fortunate winning a girl like that. Be good to her," or something of the kind.'

'Perhaps she talked to me about you. I don't remember. I don't remember anything. But—didn't I expect there to be an inquiry after Miss Carter's death—or were you expecting that at any minute?'

'If I'd been called in the next morning I should have given a certificate without any demur. It's true she might have lived another three weeks, but she might equally well have died at the end of three days. Any sudden exertion or shock—that's why we were so careful she didn't walk about her room by herself; she only had to stumble and perhaps strike her head against a chair, and that would have been sufficient to stop the heart's action. But as it happened I was out when you rang to give me the news, and Wotton insisted on sending for her own man, and he wasn't satisfied, not knowing the case, and at once all the fat was in the fire. I didn't even hear about it till you telephoned me at midday.'

She said curiously, 'How much harm did it do you? Did anyone suggest it was a put up job? I can see it would be easy to make out a case. Naturally I should count on your being the first medical man to see her, equally I should expect you to give the certificate straight away, there'd be no questions asked, and in due course we could get married and shake the dust of Ferriby Park off our feet. Tell me the truth, it's a bit late to start sparing me anything now. Did anyone suggest it was—collusion?'

'Only that fool, Ralph Carter,' muttered Dr Crane, 'He was hopping mad to lose the £9000. People found guilty of a capital crime can't inherit, you know, and I dare say he could have done with a nice lump of capital just then. But the coroner knew his job. He asked at once if he had any proof of his assertions. Ralph tried to bluster, but that didn't get him far. In a sense, you know, he did you quite a bit of good. That nasty little exhibition of malice turned public opinion against him. I even heard a whisper that he might have engineered the whole thing himself.'

'Could he have done?'

'Well, he swears he saw the tablets when he arrived, he was alone in the kitchen for a few minutes, when you and Wotton were both out of the house, the milk was there. I suppose he could have crumbled some tablets into it. We know the stuff must have been taken fairly late at night, so there's no chance that he put them into her tea cup. No, I don't think anyone thought he had done it, but at least he got you the benefit of the doubt.'

'And after that?'

'Well, after that was the funeral. You didn't go, you said you'd guard the flat, while Wotton went. In any case, you'd have been mad to go. When Wotton came back you'd disappeared. She thought you were simply out and it was late that evening before she began to get suspicious. She telephoned me to know if you were here. I said of course not, and you wouldn't go without leaving a note. I don't mind telling you, Barbara, you had me on the rack. You see, it wasn't realised at first that you'd taken any luggage. You'd left all your personal papers behind, Post Office book, cheque-book, even your insurance card. We didn't see how you could get on without that. I rang up the hospitals, but of course without result. And then . . .'

'And then the mortuaries,' she chimed in softly. 'I suppose you'd made it perfectly clear that I was dead to you in the circumstances?'

'That's not so. I told you I couldn't change overnight, but you insisted on returning my ring. I got a chap to make inquiries about bodies taken out of the river. . . .'

'But if I meant to commit suicide, why should I choose such an unpleasant way? Weren't there any sleeping-tablets left?'

'They were in the possession of the police.' His voice had gone very dry. For herself, Barbara felt as though at any moment her head would split in two; she seemed to have lost touch with any form of actuality now, couldn't identify herself with Barbara Hurst, had said good-bye to Barbara Field, and as for Barbara Fitton, well, that had been a form of theft— and against a dead girl—from the start.

'Wasn't there a gas-oven?' she asked, and her voice seemed to float away from her up to the ceiling.

'The house was all electric.'

'Someone knew all the answers, didn't they?'

'Barbara!'

'And if I had finished her, it would be ridiculous not to— draw my wages, so to speak. Nine thousand pounds is a lot of money. I could buy myself a husband with nine thousand pounds, couldn't I? But not a doctor, because they know too much.'

He caught her by the shoulders and shook her; her head bobbed like a rag doll.

'Stop playing up like this,' he said angrily. 'Aren't things bad enough? And you're going to marry no one unless you marry me. And before that time we'll get you back in your right mind and we'll solve the problem. Now that I see you again face to face I can't believe it's true. There must be some other explanation. She took the stuff herself. . . .'

'Should I accept responsibility if that were the case?'

'It would depend,' he said slowly. 'You might feel you'd driven her to it. You said a little earlier that you felt responsible for Mrs Calmady's death, because you hadn't gone straight in. Barbara, where are you staying?'

'Mr Menzies has found me a furnished flat. It's in Linton Court. I had to have some kind of headquarters. I'm going to see Wotton next—she might give me a clue without knowing she was giving it. If necessary, I'll see the nephew, too. And then, when I know the truth and know I'm not guilty, and if you still want me, I'll come back and marry you—because it'll mean I've become Barbara Hurst again, and found my love.'

She stayed a little longer, asking questions, trying to patch the answers into some sort of pattern.

'What did Miss Carter die of? No, I mean, what were you treating her for? A malignant growth? Inoperable? Did she know?'

'She may have guessed.'

'Perhaps I let it out and she decided to—to call it a day. Philip, I must go. It takes a long time to get back.'

He put his arms about her, laid his cheek against hers. She suffered this without any sense of response. It was strange to think that once the touch of his hand would have spelt rapture, that she would go on remembering his kisses, plan for a future all trained about him, as ivy writhes itself round a tree. Ivy! Ugh! A horrid simile. She didn't know why it should leap at this moment into her mind. For ivy kills. It may be picturesque, but it is death to the living plant.

He felt the long shudder run through her, and released her at once. Instantly she was full of remorse.

'It wasn't that. You don't understand. And I don't understand how you can even want to marry me while I'm under this cloud. Perhaps you and Mr Menzies are both right, it would be better to accept the situation and do nothing about it.'

'I am sure it would,' he said steadfastly. 'But if you will go ahead, at least accept the protection of my name. I'll ask no more of you than that till you're ready—I promise it. But it's as well to remember that a husband can't be subpœnaed to testify against his wife.'

'Testify? But this isn't a trial.' She was shocked at the idea.

'If you go digging about you may get the police on their toes again, and I doubt if you'll find that they will meekly accept your story of losing your memory, particularly as so many of the gaps have now been filled in by Menzies and myself. . . .'

'I'll be careful,' she promised. 'I swear I will. But I'll go and see Wotton—and Mr Menzies is keeping an eye on me. He says I'm his client, whether he likes it or not. Oh, Philip, I'm glad I came, it seems to have established another link with reality. Ah, you're a doctor, surely you can give me some hope that my memory will come back as suddenly as it went. I must have known who I was when I left the house in Ferriby Park, and I'd lost myself by the time I got to Beachampton. But that self is somewhere, looking for a place to live. . . .'

He shook his head. 'Oh my dear, I can promise you nothing. We're only on the fringe of knowledge where the kingdom of the mind is concerned. As for personality, what is it? An off-shoot of the life force, a part of an eternal power? Barbara, promise you'll keep in touch, and be very very careful. I feel you'll dissolve back into thin air as soon as you're out of my sight.'

He walked back to the station with her; it was quite dark and there was no one to recognise her or whisper under cover of a lifted hand, 'There she goes, Barbara Hurst, one of the lucky ones. And she gets the money. Nine thousand pounds.' Or nineteen. Or ninety. There never seemed any limit to speculation in cases like these.

After her train had departed he walked slowly back. He knew—had always known, he supposed—that she was always going to matter to him so long as they both lived. In a sense, his whole life had changed its shape the first day he set eyes on her, new-minted as sunlight, in old Miss Carter's drawing-room, the one young, undaunted thing in the whole set-up. And he could not, at that stage, appreciate how vastly she was going to matter to him in the weeks that lay ahead.

CHAPTER 8

Emily Wotton was a spry little woman, short and solid, with a face that looked as though it had been carved out of an outsize walnut; it was all craggy angles and the skin was a dark colour so that she always looked as if she were on the verge of an explosion. She had small suspicious lively eyes, a shapeless nose like a dab of pastry, and dark hair combed severely behind her ears. Her sister, Mrs Jessica Marsh, was a large placid woman, with white hair and an abundant bosom. They were Jack Sprat and his wife to each other, and, since they had set up under the same roof, both found life livelier than it had been for years, though neither would have admitted it. They simply never agreed about anything.

Before Em's arrival, Mrs Marsh had seemed likely to sink, by cosy degrees, into the tranquillity of the tomb, whither Mr Marsh had preceded her almost twenty years before. She was a ruminant creature, quite content with the daily round, the common task. But no one could live in supine contentment with Em. It was like opening a door to a visitor and finding it torn out of your hand by a blast. Everything connected with Em had a whirlpool quality. How old Miss Carter had stood it, Jessica couldn't imagine. But perhaps she really hadn't noticed, had wrapped herself in a cocoon of indifference that preserved her from confusion. If that had been the case, how Jessica envied her. Em drove her half-crazy sometimes. No dust lay quiet where Em was. Why, she couldn't even walk quietly, she whisked, she whirled, she flew. Drawers in her bedroom chest were rattled out and banged back; she perpetually sang hymns as she worked, always a bit off key.

My God, I love Thee, not because
I hope for Heaven thereby

bawled Em to her Maker, whizzing up and down the stairs
that creaked under her small weight. But she hoped for Heaven
just the same, Jessica noted, talking of it with a familiar assur-
ance, as though it were a theatre in which she'd booked her
seat.

Mrs Marsh was Church of England.

'Sycophantic, I call it,' sniffed Em, who rather fancied her
vocabulary. 'Just because the gentry go. You was brought up
chapel same as me, Jess.'

'Mr Marsh was Church of England,' said Jessie quietly.

'Men!' sniffed Em, who'd never had an offer, and no wonder,
reflected Mrs Marsh, who was aware of the fact. Talk about
nurturing a viper in your bosom. Em was about as restful as a
rattlesnake. Before Em came, Mrs Marsh used to drift down to
breakfast about nine o'clock and as like as not take a tray back
to bed with her.

'What's wrong with you, Jess?' demanded Em, bristling like
a devil's coachman with its tail cocked. 'If you're sick you
should see a doctor. Now we've got the Welfare State there's
no excuse about not being able to afford it.'

'I'm not ill,' defended Jessie. 'It's just that I've reached an
age when I like to take things easy.'

'Be stretched in your grave soon enough, I shouldn't wonder,'
retorted Em briskly. 'That's something else you learned from
your husband, I suppose. Apeing the gentry. . . .'

Within two weeks, no more, Jessie was meekly getting up to
breakfast every morning. It was less exhausting than confronting
Em, gibbering with indignation at the foot of the bed.

Em had very few letters; she constantly bemoaned the fact.
'Out of sight, out of mind,' she said. 'Everyone was glad enough
to see me when there was something to be got out of me.'

Jessie, on the other hand, had a good many. 'Nothing to do
but scribble, scribble all day like a mouse in the wainscot,'
scolded the derisive Em. So when one morning the younger
sister found an envelope addressed to her on the mat, she was

very mysterious about it, though she adopted an off-hand
air.

'Fancy anyone remembering I'm alive!' she observed, slitting
the envelope. 'Asking for a subscription, I suppose.'

But when she had drawn out the single close-written sheet it
contained she couldn't keep up her show of indifference.

'Well, of all the sauce!' she exclaimed. 'How she dared! The
hussy! And her a murderess!'

Jessie had meant to be very casual, too, not even notice there
was a letter, just as though Em had dozens every day. But when
she heard that expression she became as agitated as Em herself.

' Who's a murderess?' she demanded.

'How many do you suppose I know? That Barbara Hurst, of
course. Got my address from Mr Menzies and is coming down
to see me, without so much as a by-your-leave. Bringing a
poisoned dart with her, I shouldn't wonder.'

'Why should she want you out of the way?' demanded Jessie
mildly, yet with the faintest possible inflection on the third
word. And, after all, why should she? *She* didn't have to live
with Em.

'Why else should she want to come?'

'Doesn't she say?'

'Oh, a lot of rigmarole about learning the truth, as if she
didn't know it. Pretends she's lost her memory or something.
Highly convenient, I must say. If she had any sense she
wouldn't go looking for that.'

'And she's coming here?' Jessie's voice was eager with
anticipation. It was funny how, before Em came, she was never
dull, but now she'd been violently jolted out of her happy rut
she needed something to sustain her in her fresh rôle. And the
way Em had talked about that girl and the things she'd said—
well, it would arouse the curiosity of a cuttlefish.

'So she says. Coming to-day, if you please. Now, Jessie, don't
you go making a lot of extra cakes for tea because of someone
that ought to be in Madame Tussaud's by rights. Because—
she's not going to be asked to tea. She wouldn't be above
slipping something into my cup when my head was turned, just
to keep my mouth shut.'

Jessie prudently refrained from the obvious comment. 'To-day? you said.'

'That's right. And she hopes it'll be convenient, but doesn't wait for a reply. And, if it isn't, she'll camp on the doorstep till your great soft heart melts and you let her in. Well, if you find yourself dead in bed to-morrow, don't say I didn't warn you.'

Barbara came down from London by coach and caught the local bus that only ran every two hours, so that it was after three o'clock when she reached Dunromin, which was the romantic name of Mrs Marsh's house. Mrs Marsh opened the door, and the girl thought, 'But she looks kind. This can't be Wotton.' And of course it wasn't, as she realised an instant later when a little dark face, like an angry mole, poked itself over Jessie's shoulder.

'It's a wonder to me you have the nerve to show your face here,' said the owner of the mole-visage in forbidding tones.

Mrs Marsh whirled round. 'Em!'

'Oh yes, it's your house, Jessie, I know that. I've had several weeks to learn, but all the same, considering what happened at Ferriby Park. . . .'

'I thought I'd made it clear in my letter that that's why I've come, to try and find out what did happen. I've seen Mr Menzies, but, of course, he wasn't on the spot, he can only tell me what happened afterwards, and I've seen Dr Crane. . . .'

'What did he tell you? Here, we can't hold the door open all the afternoon for all the neighbours to hear us. Come in, and don't forget to wipe your feet on the mat.'

Barbara came in, accepting Jessie's silent invitation to enter the prim but comfortable parlour.

'What did Dr Crane say?'

'He told me the evidence he'd given at the inquest. . . .'

'And the robins in the fairy-tale couldn't have done more covering up than he did then,' interposed Em, looking about as friendly as a monstrous crow. 'Well—I suppose you're here to tell us you've been misjudged? Or hope we'll be able to tell you that?'

'Well, what else would you hope in my shoes?' Barbara inquired, reasonably. 'Imagine if someone walked up to you and said, "Oh, Miss Wotton, I'm so glad to see you. We've been looking for you. Did you know you'd poisoned Miss Carter?" '

'You've no call to say any such thing,' cried Wotton furiously. 'There was never a whisper—not that it would have been worth my while anyway. Twenty years of my life she had, and I get a bit of moth-eaten furniture—you needn't scowl like that, Jessie, you said yourself the foot of that chest of drawers looked as if it had gangrene—and I know for a fact she bought that wardrobe off the pavement in Westbourne Grove for a pound, she told me about it herself—and not enough, when the carriage was paid, to buy a good set of blacks. I was a lot better off when she was alive.'

'No one ever suggested it was anything to do with you,' Barbara told her. 'At least, I suppose they didn't. Everyone seemed convinced it was my work.'

She looked white and drawn and there were shadows under her eyes such as no girl of twenty-one should display. Mrs Marsh, that gentle woman who had been disappointed in her hope of children, touched her on the arm.

'Come and sit by the fire, my dear. You know Em well enough to understand that her bark's worse than her bite. No one wants to see justice done more than she does—well, of course you do, Em, you with your talk about the heavenly mansions and eternal right. If we can help you,' added Jessie, turning back to their visitor, 'you may be sure we will. And the first thing I'm going to do is put on the kettle for a nice cup of tea. Yes, Em, tea. And if you don't fancy any there's nothing to stop you making yourself a nice cup of cocoa.'

'What more did the doctor tell you?' demanded Em, as the door closed behind the busy Mrs Marsh.

'He seemed to think it would be wisest to leave things to nature, in the hope that presently things would clear themselves up, but I can't do that, Miss Wotton. It would mean going on under a cloud perhaps for years, perhaps for ever. Anything would be better than that.'

'Would it?' sniffed Wotton. 'There's some things it might be best not to remember.'

Mrs Marsh came back and, opening a drawer, took out a

linen cloth copiously embroidered and edged with hand-crocheted lace.

'You see,' the girl went on, 'I can't help feeling that if I were guilty I wouldn't want to discover the truth. Would I?' she repeated desperately.

'Of course not, dear,' agreed Jessie, spreading the cloth on the table.

'That's the best tablecloth,' observed Em, accusingly.

'It's the one we always have when there's company. Sit back in that chair, Miss Hurst. It's not going to bite you. This Dr Crane never thought you did it, you know.'

'That's what he *said*,' corrected Em.

'If he does think so he should be ashamed of himself. Engaged to marry you and all.'

'He's still ready to marry me,' cried Barbara unguardedly. 'But, of course,' she went on, seeing Em's scandalised face, 'I can't. I won't risk my children . . .'

'Well, really,' expostulated Em, turning pink, 'no need to talk about them yet. Time for that when you've got your lines. Well now, what is it you think I can do to help you?'

'Tell me what happened that last day so far as you know. Oh yes, I've heard what Mr Menzies had to say and Dr Crane, but they don't know much. You were there all the time. Indeed, go back farther than that, tell me something about myself. Who was I before I came to Miss Carter? Worked in a hat shop that went bankrupt, Mr Menzies told me. But—haven't I any relations?'

'Oh, you're flotsam all right,' Em assured her grimly. ''Vacuated to the country when you were five, your daddy was killed in the war. . . .'

'And my mother?'

'She didn't show up much, never sent coupons for clothes or anything. Mind you, she was in London all through the blitz and a lot of people that were killed were never identified, and she didn't put in for her ration book after about '43, so it could be she was one of the unlucky ones. Anyhow, this Mrs Trent kept you—no children of her own, see—and you stayed with her till you were about sixteen. Then she died and presently you came up to London and got this job with a hat shop. Lived in and made yourself useful till that went west, too, and then you answered Miss Carter's advertisement for a useful companion-help.'

'I couldn't have produced much in the way of references. What made her take me?'

'Well, to tell you the truth,' said Em, unbending slightly, 'there wasn't all that competition. She could be difficult, you know. Why, Miss Benedict, the one before you, told her she'd sooner be maid to a female dragon. But you,' she acknowledged grudgingly, 'you seemed to get on with her from the first. Used to take her out shopping in her bath-chair, read to her by the hour together—her sight wasn't what it had been, you see, and you get sick of that everlasting wireless. Used to beat me sometimes she didn't get tired of hearing your voice, but no, on and on you'd go.'

'I must have been happy then or I wouldn't have stayed. I could have got something.'

'Maybe you knew when you were well off. I was there, you see, and it isn't every house that has someone else to do the washing-up. Besides, she was old and there was the money, and she had no relatives except the nephew and she hated him like poison. He wouldn't have got a penny of hers if she could have prevented it. Oh no, you had your head screwed on all right. And then there was the doctor. Fair threw yourself at his head, you did.'

'Em!' exclaimed Mrs Marsh, who had gone out to wet the tea and came back just in time to hear the last sentence.

'Well, the girl wants the truth, doesn't she? Mind you, he was the sort that was used to that kind of thing. Anyhow, you and him were going to be married.'

'Did Miss Carter know?'

'She'd have to be blind not to. Oh yes, she knew.'

'And she didn't disapprove?'

'Once she was gone it wouldn't matter to her what you did, and it was part of the arrangement you only got the money if you stayed with her till she died.'

'And—she hadn't given me notice or anything?'

'If you don't remember, I'm sure I don't. She never spoke of such a thing to me.'

'And yet she was proposing to cut me out of her will. Is that the fact?'

'I can only tell you what I know. That last day she didn't seem herself at all. The doctor came in unexpected-like and he noticed there was something wrong, but of course I couldn't tell him anything. At that age you don't expect to feel spry every morning. You'd gone out shopping, and presently Miss Carter said to me to ring Mr Menzies, but not a word to you. You wouldn't have known either, but I couldn't get the number. Three times I tried and the third time you came back while I was on the line. The dining-room door was open, you couldn't help but hear.'

'And she didn't give you any hint why she wanted to change her will, if that's really what she had in mind.'

'She had that in mind all right. "I've been deceived right along," she said, "and not for the first time. Experience seems such a waste, if it doesn't teach you anything."'

'What on earth did she mean by that?'

'She was courted when she was a girl and found out just in time that the chap was after what she had rather than what she was. I suppose she thought this was history repeating itself, and you were counting your chickens before they were hatched.'

'I don't believe she thought anything of the kind,' exclaimed Barbara.

'Well, she had some reason.'

She closed her jaws like a praying mantis—snap, snap.

'Go on,' said Barbara impatiently.

'There isn't any more. Mr Menzies never got there in time.'

Mrs Marsh passed the scones. 'Take two, dear, they're ever so small. Go on, Em. We're both waiting.'

'I told you, there isn't any more. Mr Ralph came in that afternoon, he was staying in London for a few days, and Miss Carter said something about the vultures gathering. Out of the Bible I think it was, though she didn't spend much time reading that, as a rule. Trashy novels by the hour together. You went off to the hairdresser. Never was any love lost between you and Mr Ralph.'

'And she told him about the lawyer coming?'

'Yes. But not to hope for anything for himself, she said.'

'She didn't tell him what she did mean to do?'

'Not likely. Why should she?'

'Then there isn't any proof she meant to cut me off.'

'You were the one she'd left the money to, weren't you?'

'And that's all the proof there is?'

'If there'd been any more you wouldn't be here now,' Wotton assured her.

'You might as well say it was my fault the hat shop went bankrupt, that I'd cooked the books or something. I suppose nobody did say that?'

'I couldn't say, I'm sure,' returned Em, putting her stubby nose in the air.

'There's times, Em,' intervened Mrs Marsh in a spirited voice, 'I think it's a pity you didn't get yourself married. It 'ud have learned you a lot. I'll tell you this, my girl. Your nose wouldn't be the shape it is now if you'd turned it up at a husband the way you're turning it up at Miss Hurst. And it might have looked better,' she wound up, breathlessly.

Em couldn't believe her ears. If the table had got up and bitten her she couldn't have been more startled. 'Well, really, Jessie,' she said, 'taking sides against your own sister like that.'

'You must excuse my sister, Miss Hurst,' said the impenitent Jessie. 'She was always a trouble-maker even as a little girl. I'm sure I wish there was something I could do to help, and if you do marry this Dr Crane all I can say is he's a very lucky man.'

'You're welcome to your opinion,' retorted Em stiffly.

'Proof's one thing and common sense is another,' persisted Jessie. 'Anyone could see Miss Hurst isn't the kind that would go round poisoning old ladies. No, you mark my words, either she took it herself in a sort of coma-like or that nephew did it. Now, Em, it's no good going back on your own words. If you've said once he had a murderous look in his eye you've said it twenty times.'

'Are you thinking of going to see Mr Ralph?' Em inquired of the girl. 'Mind you, it's a long way.'

Barbara seemed suddenly dispirited. 'I don't know that it would be any good. If I didn't even see him that afternoon there's nothing he could tell me that he hasn't said already. Of course we don't know what he may have said to Miss Carter, but from all I've heard it doesn't seem likely she'd take the stuff herself.'

'Not with her lawyer coming down the next morning,' agreed the grim Miss Wotton.

Barbara left soon afterwards, not feeling she'd achieved very much. No one could suggest why she should have gone to Beachampton, unless it was because of Miss Carter's sister having lived there and Miss Carter talking about her and the asylum, which was really what it was, till the cows came home, and it didn't seem as though she could have booked at a hotel, or why was her bag at the station? Since she couldn't believe in her own guilt, that only left the nephew, and she couldn't see any possibility of proving he was responsible. Not that she wanted anyone to hang, she was only too eager to put the whole affair behind her, but how could she till she was satisfied in her own mind that *she* wasn't responsible?

'Even Philip thinks in his heart I did it,' she decided.

Menzies had thought the same, but then he was a lawyer and had to work on facts, and she supposed that, if she were an outsider instead of an interested party, she might take the same point of view.

The local bus went for the last time at 5.45. If she missed that she'd be stranded for the night, so, thanking Mrs Marsh for her hospitality, and saying good-bye to Em as cautiously as if she were a man-eater, she walked down the path into the country lane.

The world seemed quite empty once she was past the few cottages; her footsteps echoed on the road till it seemed as though someone was following her. But she put that silly idea behind her. The bus stop was a little green triangle with a sign-post in it, with three arms, two of which said No Through Road.

A wind came past shaking the leaves; the sky cuddled down on the distant woods. Time passed.

The bus was overdue, five minutes, then ten. She began to get nervous; if she missed the London-bound coach it meant an hour until the next one. Twenty minutes past its time the bus rolled up. The conductor hadn't arrived and they'd had to send for a substitute. Barbara got in asking hopefully, 'Will you be able to make up the time?' because if not, what would she do?

She had no idea she was proceeding towards one of the most momentous encounters of her life.

CHAPTER 9

Mr Arthur Crook of 123 Bloomsbury Street and 2 Brandon Street, Earls Court, London, following his normal avocation of lawyer-cum-amateur-sleuth, came driving through the deserted village of Amberfield and over the hill to Whytebough. There didn't seem any traffic about, which suited him admirably. He had no use at all for the country, and would have supported a ten-pound-a-week minimum wage for agricultural workers as compensation for having to live in a world of fields and trees, away from the cosy lights and the noise and unending excitement of the metropolis. A Green coach shone its rear lights for an instant at the corner ahead, hesitated by a request stop and went on. About a minute later a local bus drew up a few yards behind and a girl came pounding out and ran towards the coach stop, though she must have known it was a waste of energy since the coach was already disappearing over the skyline. There was something about her stance and general bearing that troubled him. No one so young had a right to look so dejected simply because of a missed bus. He remembered the old saying: Never run for a train or a woman, there'll always be another coming along.

There was a cold nip in the air and a suggestion of fog, though he hoped to reach London before that presented a serious consideration. As he drew alongside the coach stop he slowed down his high-bodied bright yellow Rolls, that attracted attention wherever it went, and sticking an immense red face, crowned by a check cap of deplorable pattern, out of the window, he called, 'Goin' my way?'

The girl looked startled, but that didn't bother him. They all

114

did at the first time of meeting, but they soon got used to him in the way you get accustomed to a creaking board on the stairs or a garishly-painted sign over your favourite inn.

'I want to go to London,' she faltered.

'Who doesn't?' He opened the door of the car. 'Hop' in, sugar. The Old Superb and me'll beat your coach to it or my name's not Arthur Crook.'

She was very quiet and pale, but that didn't distress him unduly, because people in trouble were his business. The healthy and sane and secure ones could get along very well without him, and nobody appreciates being overlooked.

'Had a nice day in the country?' he asked politely in a kind voice—because it takes all sorts to make a world and that's some people's idea of pleasure.

'I didn't come down to have a nice day, exactly,' she confessed.

'Visiting an old aunt?'

'Not even that.'

He shot her an appraising, professional glance. 'Crook's the name,' he announced. 'Arthur Crook and trouble is my business. Hang on to this.' He flicked a card out of his pocket. It was the biggest visiting card she had ever seen, and when she had read it she understood why. It had so much to say. *No reasonable offer refused*, it read. *Day and night service. We only work for the innocent*. Hesitatingly she pushed it back to him.

'Put it in your pouch,' offered Mr Crook in friendly tones. 'Never know when it may come in useful. Not that I'm touting for custom, mind you. It 'ud surprise you to know how many mountains uproot themselves to visit this Mahomet. But the best of us can get into the red through no fault of our own. Don't they tell us the ways of Providence are not our ways? I'll say!' he wound up, feelingly.

He didn't have to look in her direction to recognise the sudden change that transformed her during the latter part of his speech.

'You do believe in Providence?' she asked eagerly.

He shrugged enormous shoulders, clad in the brightest brown suit she had ever beheld.

115

'Call it fate, luck, anything you please, I ain't particular. Now, sugar, it could be I'm wrong, but I generally find what you might term a chance encounter has some meaning.' Or else he invested it with one, he might have added. It was a pretty safe bet, anyway. Sooner or later everybody got into trouble, and the lucky ones crossed his path. If you didn't—get into trouble, he meant—the odds were you were a cabbage and the sooner you went back to Mother Earth, leaving your share of food and living-space to more enterprising folk, the better. Because no man liveth to himself alone, and it was his experience that a good many didn't die to themselves alone either. And it was then that he came in. Not that he could carry the troubles of the whole human race, naturally. His day only contained 24 hours like everyone else's, and he made 'em all work overtime. Sometimes his clients were up in the seventies before they so much as heard of his name; others, they were in the bloom of youth like this girl. Personally, he didn't care, except that he generally got more help from the oldsters. Come to that, he'd have served a skeleton if it had put its head out of its grave and appealed to him.

'I wonder,' said the girl, and now there was a note of hope in her voice, 'if you could help me. Because it's true. I'm in terrible trouble.'

'Then I'm your man,' replied Crook sensibly, swerving to avoid a Citroen that came over the hump of the hill in the middle of the road doing a rash forty-five. 'Start at the beginning and go on till I stop you. Just mention your name,' he added, encouragingly, 'and the nature of your business.'

When he heard it was Murder he could have hugged himself, her, too, for that matter. In a field of likely runners it always carried his money.

She began her story, hesitatingly at first, as if she scarcely expected to be believed; he stopped her now and again, demanding clarification of some detail, checking up a time or a statement. When presently she fell silent he looked at her in surprise.

'That the end? Or have you forgotten the rest?'

116

'I was just thinking—hearing myself talk it must sound so improbable I can hardly ask you to believe it.'

'What price the faith that moves mountains? As a matter of fact, I was thinking it was just up my street. I do like a bit of enterprise, and you'd be astonished to know how many people tell the same story with nothing altered but the names. Like these store detectives. They get sick and tired of the monotony of the excuses they hear. *I didn't notice what I'd done. I don't know how that came to be in my bag. I never did anything like that before.* I thought I knew all the bundle, but this is nice and fresh. What were you thinking of doing now?'

'I had thought of going to see Ralph Carter, but I don't know whether it would be much use. I couldn't argue with anything he chose to say, because I don't know where the truth lies. If he said he had nothing to do with it, well how could I contradict him?'

'Maybe you couldn't, but you'll be surprised at what I can do. Remember Artemus Ward, wasn't it? Get the evidence and then arrange it the way it suits you best. Where does the fellow live?'

'Up in the Lake District. I've got the address. But he hasn't any motive. Dr Crane agrees with me.'

'All you both mean is you don't know of any motive. Come to that, maybe he doesn't right now, but he'll be astounded to find how much motive he had by the time I've finished with him. There's no reason I can see why he shouldn't have doctored the milk, and before I'm through with him he'll be wondering if he really did.'

As far as Mr Crook was concerned trains need never have been invented. He would cheerfully have sold British Railways to the scrap merchants and never have noticed it had disappeared. His fantastic car, the Old Superb, that had replaced the famous little red Scourge, heroine of twenty similar adventures, carried him triumphantly up to the north, remarked wherever she went. When he had reached his destination he didn't go straight to Ralph Carter's house. He found an easy-looking local in the neighbourhood and wandered into the Public Bar soon after opening time when there wouldn't be

117

a crowd, and he could look for a little personal attention.

'If you want to know what's bein' said in the neighbourhood, try the Public Bar,' was always his advice.

He ordered a pint, opened his uvula and lowered it in one mighty draught. The barman looked at him with respect and hastened to refill his tankard.

'Staying long in these parts, sir?' he asked.

'Just passing through,' Crook assured him. 'Know a man called Carter, Ralph Carter?'

From the changed expression on the man's face it was simple to deduce that Mr Carter was not very popular in the local.

'Doesn't do us much good, see,' the landlord, who acted as his own barman at this hour of the evening, assured Crook. 'Comes in now and again, but mostly if someone else is paying. Is it him you've come north to see?'

'That's right. Missed him when he was down in London a few weeks back.'

'So he was,' Bob Tanner recalled. 'His auntie died. Bit of a shemozzle there, by all accounts.'

'Really?' Crook looked as interested as a bright terrier when someone mentions rats. 'Why, he didn't murder her or anything, did he?'

The landlord, arrested in his movement towards the beer-handle, looked wary.

'I never heard that said, but there was an inquest, so they tell us.'

'What happened? Auntie fall off a cliff?'

'She was an old lady,' said Bob reprovingly. 'No, but there was a young woman in the household, hadn't been there much above a year, I understand, and it came out she got most of the money.'

'And couldn't wait for Nature to take its course? What happened to her?'

'She got the money,' was Bob's simple reply. 'Mr Carter he was fit to be tied. What's the good of having a police force, he said, when they let murderers slip between their fingers?'

'Hold hard!' exclaimed Crook. 'Quite sure he said that?'

'In this very bar. Leastways, in the Saloon. He don't come into the Public.'

'Silly fellow,' murmured Crook indulgently. 'All the same, he should mind his tongue. The young lady could bring an action against him if he goes round the countryside accusing her of murder.'

'Funny you should say that,' commented Bob. 'The colonel was in the Saloon that night and he turned to Mr Carter and said, "If you've got proof there's been a murder committed you should go to the police. And if you haven't you should keep your trap shut. Unless, of course, you want to find yourself faced with an action for slander."'

'I couldn't have put it better myself,' Crook approved.

'After Mr Carter had gone, and he didn't stop long, I can tell you, the colonel said, "I wouldn't care to be in the young lady's shoes if her path and Carter's cross again." If anyone ever looked like murder, that's the fellow.'

'Never a dull moment!' approved Crook. He didn't stay much longer, and soon asked if he could get a room for the night.

'Well, we don't have accommodation here, I'm sorry to say, though we could put up your car, if you liked. But Mrs Gugg in the village generally has a room, very clean and you can leave your change on the dressing-table and not bother to count it when you come back.'

'Suits me,' said Crook, so leaving the Old Superb at the Dying Duck, he marched down the little village street and called on Mrs Gugg. She registered the usual surprise at first sight of him, but the mention of Bob Tanner cleared her doubts. She said it was a nice bright room and she did a full breakfast. Crook said he was a lawyer from London who had business with a local big job called Ralph Carter. Mrs Gugg pursed her lips from which he deduced that Ralph wasn't such a big job as he liked to think, and then said it was all over the place that Mr Carter's auntie had died sudden and he'd been cheated out of a fortune by a designing harpy, who'd terrified the old lady into leaving her all her money and then poisoned her. And how people got away with these things—well, don't ask Mrs Gugg.

'Mustn't believe all you hear,' Crook warned her sunnily, 'and take it from me, you're goin' to hear quite a lot in the next few days.'

Ralph Carter was standing by the front window of the unpretentious and ugly little house he had called The Firs, when he saw a fantastic bright yellow car draw up at his gate. He called out facetiously to Maisie, his wife, who matched him in every way, in temperament, greed and a figure that could have come straight out of a modern sculpture exhibition. 'They're running the Old Crocks' Race in the north nowadays, it seems. Come and take a look.' Maisie came and saw someone as like a gorilla as any human being could hope to be hop agilely out of the yellow monstrosity and make for the gate. She was in two minds as to whether to let him in. Officially she had a woman in the mornings, but the girl, as she persisted in calling her, had walked out the previous week and not yet been replaced. All Maisie's girls did this sooner or later, their north-country independence rebelling against her southern snoopiness.

'I'll soon send him to rightabouts,' said Ralph in a lordly way, marching into the little hall. 'Probably wants to borrow the telephone.'

He kept a red tin pig on the hall-table, with a slit in its back for the coppers of lost or bewildered travellers. When Crook first saw it he felt an involuntary stab of respect for the man, because a fellow who could choose so apposite a money-box must have good in him somewhere.

'Mr Carter? Okey-doke. Crook's the name, Arthur Crook, and I represent Miss Barbara Hurst.'

Ralph, who had been about to close the door, suddenly froze. 'What's that you said?'

'You 'eard.' Crook lugged a card out of his pocket, not the generous affair he had offered Barbara but a much more discreet production. From it the shocked Ralph discovered he was talking to a member of the legal profession—and he must have got by in the dark on a thick night, thought Mr Carter resentfully—and, believe it or not, he was here on Barbara's behalf.

Crook proceeded to make himself at home, tossing his appalling check cap on top of a yet more appalling fake oak chest.

'Miss Hurst,' repeated Ralph, to give himself time to think.

'Your late auntie's companion. Surely you hadn't forgotten? You seem to have been spreadin' some very rum stories locally about the young lady.'

Ralph stiffened. He'd been a major once and he never forgot it, and he certainly wasn't going to take insolence from a fellow who wore such a cap and drove such a car.

'I've a perfect right to express an opinion,' he exclaimed.

'Don't you believe it, chum. Not in this day and age. Why, you could be as easy hanged by red tape as the hang-man's necktie, and that's the word of the chap who knows.'

Maisie, attracted by a snatch of this conversation, came to the door of the lounge, as they called their single sitting-room. They were terribly modern and American, they explained to everyone, and ate in the kitchen.

'Who is it, Ralph?'

'You'd better come in,' said Ralph painfully to Crook. 'It's Barbara Hurst making more trouble,' he told his wife bitterly.

'I should have expected her to be glad to lie low,' was Maisie's spirited rejoinder. 'It's obvious to everyone she was responsible for your aunt's death. . . .'

'Not to me it ain't,' Crook assured her. 'Nor it wasn't to a coroner's jury, and before I'm through it's goin' to be equally clear to everyone else or my name ain't Arthur Crook, and seeing it's been that for more than half a century . . .'

Ralph looked dazed by this attack, but Maisie showed more spirit. 'You go back and tell Barbara Hurst that she can't except to have nine thousand pounds and a good name,' she said.

'You haven't been about enough,' Crook retorted. 'Quite a lot of people manage to have both.'

'And I shall never believe she doesn't know a great deal more about my aunt's death than she chose to tell the court,' Ralph broke in, recovering his powers of speech.

'Surprise you to know that at the moment she don't know anything at all? Fact. All this tamasha brought on a sort of breakdown. She disappeared after the funeral, and turned up at a place called Beachampton on the South Coast, not even rememberin' how she got there or who she was. When she met this fellow, Menzies—a colleague of mine,' he added airily, 'she was callin' herself Barbara Field. He was able to tell her who she was and the shock nearly gave her another breakdown. I'm here to find out what really happened.'

'Then you've had a very long journey for nothing,' exclaimed Maisie, quick as light. 'My husband told the coroner all he knew; and he wasn't even in the house when Miss Carter died.'

'Too true. But he was there that afternoon. And I'm here to make sure that the evidence he gave was all Sir Garnet.'

'If you're suggesting perjury,' shouted Ralph, and his wife intervened: 'Send for the police. He pushed his way in, it's practically housebreaking. . . .'

'Send for the whole of Scotland Yard—if they'll come,' agreed Crook. 'And no one's mentioned perjury. Only—anybody can make a mistake and if you tell me you can't I'll know you're not human. Now, everything hinges on this phial of tablets that disappeared so suddenly the night Miss Carter died. You told the coroner you saw it during the afternoon?'

'Yes.' Ralph sounded defiant.

'According to Miss Hurst it was missing when she went to look for it in the evening. No one else had been in the room, except the old lady herself, of course, and it don't seem likely she could have hidden it. I mean, even if she'd taken the tablets out, what about the phial?'

'In any case, why should she?'

'Why indeed? Now, I understand you were sortin' papers all the afternoon.'

'Yes.'

'So it's possible, ain't it, that the phial could have got mixed up and shoved into a waste-paper basket, unbeknownst?' His voice was almost pleading.

'I consider that most unlikely. The phial was on a table beside the bed and personally I never handled it.'

'Then—tell me this—are you prepared to swear, *on oath if need be*, and it could come to that, that the phial and tablets were there when you left the room for the last time?'

'Seeing I hadn't touched them . . .'

'That ain't what I asked.'

Ralph was beginning to look a little intimidated; he was a biggish man with a mud-coloured complexion, who physically had run to seed. An apprehensive look now began to cloud his heavy face. It was Maisie who answered.

'Of course he's sure.'

Crook turned to her politely. 'No one told me you were there, Mrs Carter. You mean, you can alibi your husband's statement? Well, that's fine. Better, of course, if you weren't his wife. The law's so cynical. It don't believe a husband's or wife's word is conclusive. If Mr Carter's lookin' for an alibi . . .'

'Why on earth should I require an alibi?' demanded Ralph, rather too loudly.

'I was comin' to that. Now, you remember the phial was there when you arrived; you're dead sure it didn't get thrown away with the garbage; and yet it wasn't there when Miss Hurst wanted it that evening. So the suggestion's bound to be made that it went away same time as you did. Now, keep your hair on,' he implored, as Ralph began to make stuttering noises indicative of indignation. 'We've none of us got so much at our time of life we can afford to lose any—just put yourself in my place and see what other solution you'd offer to frank a client.'

'You are suggesting my husband—*my husband*—had something to do with Miss Carter's death?' Maisie's voice was as shrill as a cormorant.

'It don't matter a button to me who put out the old lady's light so long as I can show it wasn't my client.' Crook had explained this so often in various cases that he seriously thought of having a gramophone record made that he could play at the appropriate moment. 'But though I can make bricks with as little straw as any man livin', even I need a little. And, frankly, I can't see a motive for anyone outside the family, so to speak, wanting to make trouble, even if there was any opportunity. And at the present moment I don't even see who else had the opportunity. Now—I understand the old lady was alone for a bit during the afternoon.'

'While I made the tea—yes.'

'Went into the kitchen?'

'That's correct.'

'And the milk for Miss Carter's nightcap was all poured out handy in a glass in the larder, and the larder opens off the kitchen—correct?'

'Er—yes, I believe it does. But I had no occasion to go into the larder, and so I never saw the milk. Wotton had left a plate of bread-and-butter cut on the kitchen table, and put out a cake and some scones on a contraption called, I believe, a curate's delight.'

'Curate's aid in my part of the world,' amended Crook sunnily. 'Still, a rose by any other name . . . Now, you were alone there?'

'Seeing that there was no one else in the flat except my aunt, who was confined to bed, I don't know who else you'd expect to be there.'

'Well, I didn't really,' said Crook.

'Are you trying to say my husband may have put the tablets in the milk?' demanded a scandalised Maisie.

'I didn't say so. What I'm trying to do is point out that there are other solutions beside the one you've accepted. Mind you, I can't prove that anyone else doctored the stuff before Miss Hurst came back, but no one else can prove that she did, and if I can show there was a chance it was someone else . . .'

'You wouldn't care how hard you hit below the belt,' wound up Maisie.

Crook gave her a grateful glance. 'Got it in one. Now, let's get this point cleared up and then I can go away and leave you in peace. Are you prepared to go into a witness-box and tell a jury that the tablets were actually on the table when you left the flat? And, if you are so prepared, can you prove beyond all reasonable doubt that they were the sleeping-pills?'

'What on earth else could they be?' Ralph sounded dumbfounded.

'I don't know. I don't know what else she took. Maybe she

124

had Aspirins or digestive tablets or peppermints. Did you notice what they were like?'

'Not particularly,' stammered Ralph. 'They just looked like tablets to me.'

'Colour?'

'Or—er—white, so far as I could see.'

'And if I tell you the sleeping-tablets were sulphur colour. . . .'

'I tell you, I can't swear to it. They looked to me white, just as the tube looked white. I didn't pick it up, and I don't remember Aunt Harriet referring to them.'

'Did it have a label or anything on it? Doctor's name? Chemist's name?'

If he had intended to rattle his companion he had succeeded. Ralph was developing a pinched look round the mouth and the nostrils.

'I tell you, I never examined it, I never touched it.'

'And anyhow, you'd hardly expect him to remember details after all this time,' chimed in Maisie loyally. 'We've all had plenty on our minds these last weeks. And I never heard that Aunt Harriet had any other sort of pills.'

'Maybe you didn't ask,' suggested Crook simply. 'And in a case of suspected murder not remembering ain't a very good answer in the witness-box, if it comes to that. Mean to say, that's no way to impress a jury.'

'He impressed a jury all right at the inquest,' stormed Maisie.

'As to that, I wasn't there, I wouldn't know. But, since we're all goin' in for plain speakin,' he ain't impressing me at this present moment. Now let's have a straight answer—yes or no. Are you or are you not prepared to swear that the tablets you saw were Miss Carter's sleeping-tablets? And if the answer's in the affirmative, how come you are so sure?'

'I've told you already, there was a tube there and it seemed reasonable to assume they were the tablets in question. All through the inquiry there's never been a suggestion they could be anything else, no one's ever suggested such a thing, I can't swear I saw them as I left but I'm absolutely sure they weren't thrown away with the rubbish. Miss Hurst says they'd vanished when she came on the scene, and so she rang up the doctor for a fresh supply. So far as I can see, there's nothing whatever to substantiate her statement.'

'Ditto, ditto, Brother Smut,' quoted Crook cheerfully.

He gave a huff and a puff that nearly made the irate Maisie Carter fall off her chair, and if she had—oh, what a fall was there, my countrymen, reflected the unrepentant Mr Crook. Then he delivered judgment.

'Fact is, your evidence ain't worth a row of beans.'

'But what does it all add up to?' Maisie demanded.

Crook's red brows, as thick as a hedge above popping brown eyes, lifted in astonishment.

'Don't you see, if the phial your husband saw wasn't the sleeping-tablets then there's no proof they hadn't been removed *before he came.*'

'Who on earth would want to do that?'

'I give you three guesses,' offered Crook generously.

'You can't mean Wotton. What on earth would she stand to gain?'

'Not having met the lady yet, can't say. But money ain't the only motive for sudden death, though it may be the most usual one. Mind you, I ain't bringing any accusation against her, not at this stage. She may be so snow-white she'd make an angel look as though he'd just walked in out of a fog. Only—if you didn't see them, they weren't there, and if they weren't there it was because someone had removed them. And if you did see them and they'd gone when Miss Hurst came to look, then they must have gone out with you. You can't have it all ways. You pays your money and you takes your choice.'

'There's a third alternative,' insisted Maisie.

'Meaning the old lady could have taken them herself? But she couldn't have swallowed the phial. No, that cock won't fight.'

'I didn't mean that at all, as you very well know. I meant, Barbara Hurst could and most likely did administer the overdose that night.'

Crook shook his big head. 'That's another non-combatant,'

he said. 'Y'see, she's my client, and I only work for the innocent.'

'That won't get you far. After all, she had the motive. . . .'

'Who says so?'

'If Miss Carter was going to change her will she's the only person likely to suffer. She was the only legatee to all intents and purposes.'

'Old lady didn't happen to mention her intentions to you, of course,' Crook suggested to Carter.

'She simply said she didn't want to wear herself out as she was seeing Menzies the next morning. I said, I hope you're not having any trouble, is there anything I can do to help? I wasn't coming north till the evening—and she said nothing she couldn't deal with. All the same, there was something wrong.'

'She didn't hint to you that your prospects might be improved?'

Ralph looked sulky. 'If you must know, she said it's never wise to begin counting chickens from sterile eggs.'

'Well, she couldn't have put it more clearly than that, could she?'

'So, you see,' continued Ralph as though he hadn't spoken, 'I had no conceivable motive for wishing to shorten her life.'

'Just one more point,' said Crook. 'There's been a lot of talk about Menzies and the will, but I haven't got a witness yet to prove it was the will she meant to discuss.'

Both the Carters stared at him as though he was some freak at a fun fair.

'What else could it conceivably have been? Of course it was the will.'

'No of course about it. There was that murmur of hers about being deceived—she never offered any explanation of that, did she? Well, I think if she'd had the chance of seein' Menzies we might be a lot less in the dark.'

'I can assure you *I* have never deceived her.' Ralph's voice was very stiff.

'Might have done it without meanin' it. Suppose she's suddenly discovered you're not her nephew (and therefore her part-heir) after all, but one of these Found-on-a-doorstep-half-past-nine-done-up-in-a-basket-tied-with-twine affairs? No, I dare say you've got your certificates, you could prove things up to the hilt, but maybe there was something else she'd just learned. I don't know. All I'm saying is you can't go jumping over the moon like the cow in the nursery rhyme and say you know she meant to change her will and that 'ud mean deprivin' Miss Hurst of part of all her inheritance, when the fact is you don't know anything of the sort. Why, you haven't got a grain of proof, not a sausage. There's skeletons in every cupboard, remember, and I don't know why you should expect to be an exception to the rule.'

From the sudden pallor perceptible in Ralph's cheeks he began to wonder if he'd chucked a stone at a gooseberry bush and brought down the moon.

'Isn't he married to that dollymop of his?' he wondered unchivalrously. 'Did he once forge a cheque? Does he peddle drugs?' Oh, the possibilities were endless.

On his return to London he put his ally, Bill Parsons, on to uncovering anything he could about Carter and his wife, while he himself went 'on the wings of the morning' as he poetically expressed it to see that old battle-axe, Emily Wotton.

CHAPTER 10

Since her retirement to Dunromin, Wotton had been mortified to learn how true is the proverb that absence makes the heart grow fonder—of another. When she was in Miss Carter's employ, many had been the afternoon that some chapel crony had dropped in with her knitting for the savages of Boorioboolaga and a copy of the *Heavenly News*. Now that she was exiled, as she feelingly put it, no one came at all, except for a few poor old pussy-cats for the metaphorical saucers of milk the good-natured Jessie would put down for any stray. Wotton sometimes wondered whether the grave mightn't prove more entertaining.

So, when one afternoon she saw an old-fashioned, high-waisted bright yellow monstrosity calling itself a car stop at the gate, it never occurred to her this could be a social call.

'I'll go, Jessie,' she announced. 'It's someone advertising—some new soap powder, I dare say. Well, we do very well with the old sort.'

But Jessie would have admitted even someone advertising a new kind of soap powder; she closed the door on no one. 'All part of the same world, aren't we?' she'd say. She was that curious creature, a woman who loved her fellows, finding them both interesting and virtuous because it never occurred to her they could be anything else.

'You're a fool, Jessie,' Em would rebuke her, and Jessie would reply mildly that in Tom's day they'd always kept open house, and you can't teach an old dog new tricks.

Mr Crook came bustling up the path as though the bears were after him.

'It's for you, Em,' said Jessie, and in came Mr Crook, beaming like an advertisement for the soap powder he didn't represent.

'Miss Wotton? Crook's the name, Arthur Crook. Acting for Miss Hurst in this unpleasant affair of Miss Carter's death. Nasty rumours goin' round, and it's my job to scotch them. I mean to say, she don't want to stay Miss Hurst for the rest of her life. . . .'

'After Dr Crane again, is she?' asked Wotton at her most disagreeable. 'Well, he's had an escape, if you ask me.'

'I wasn't,' explained Crook sunnily. 'And I don't agree anyhow. A pretty girl and nine thousand pounds—who does the chap think he is? Sir Bernard's elder brother? Now, I don't want to detain you and I can see just how much you're longin' to detain me. I know, too, how busy the ladies always are, and don't make a cuppa for me,' he added to the hospitable Jessie, turning on her his most seductive alligator grin. 'I don't know how it is, but my stomach's allergic to tea. Always was. Now, Miss Wotton, I've just come from seein' Major Carter, and he's told me something very interesting.'

Even Wotton wasn't proof against this bait. 'He said plenty at the trial.'

'Inquest,' Crook corrected. 'Any idea, by the way, why he's so anxious to see my client gaoled?'

'Because of the money, I suppose. He's always thought it should come to him. She hasn't anyone else to leave it to, he used to tell me—never thought of me, of course—and blood's thicker than water. Well, that may be so, but it's also a deal nastier.'

'Any idea if he had something to hide that she might have found out?'

'Wouldn't surprise me a bit, but if you're asking me what it was, I can't help you.'

'No hints dropped casual-like?' asked Crook wistfully.

'If there had been you can be sure I wouldn't have missed them.'

'Pity. Now, it seems as if the trouble only started the day she died. She didn't have any telephone calls?'

'The telephone wasn't in use that morning at all, neither in nor out—not till I rung up Mr Menzies after the doctor had gone, that is.'

'Can you remember if there were any letters?'

'Yes, but nothing special.'

'Remember what they were?'

'A letter from Mr Ralph saying he'd be coming that afternoon—never a word about its being convenient—letter from old Miss Turner, nothing there, just the usual So-sorry-I-haven't - been - able - to - come - to - see - you - dear - you - are - always - in - my - thoughts - I - am - in - bed-with-a-cold—real waste of a stamp, I call it, a prescription from Dr Crane that he'd promised to send the day before, the account for the gas—and if that's the best a nationalised industry can do, with the pressure something shocking directly the weather gets cold . . .'

'Ho, boatman, stem the flowing tide,' declaimed Crook. 'Hold everything, sugar. Now, did Miss Carter seem particularly put out by any of the letters?'

'Well, it was after she'd read them she sent Miss Hurst out; and later on she told me to ring Mr Menzies.'

'Didn't say anything?'

'Only the bit about being deceived.'

'Mr Ralph give any reason for his sudden call?'

'Said there were some papers he was bringing along for her to look at.'

'And you never caught sight of them? No, of course not. And by the time you came back they'd gone. What happens to the rubbish?'

'I put it all on the tradesman's lift and Hill, that's the porter, winds it down first thing and puts it in the bins, what he doesn't burn, that is. Dustman comes on a Thursday. Don't know if Dr Crane might be able to help you,' she added. 'He said to me he hoped the nephew wouldn't try her beyond her strength. She's not quite so well this morning, he said, something on her mind perhaps. Something on mine, I told him. Nothing to Mr Ralph, of course, that it was my afternoon and evening off, and that Miss Hurst was going to the hairdresser—girls washed their own hair when I was a girl. But now everything's different.'

'If ever you think of adopting a crest,' suggested Crook in friendly tones, 'I'd say a blunt instrument rampant. Say anything else—the doctor, I mean?'

'Asked where Miss Hurst was, as bold as brass. Then I heard Miss Carter calling and she told me to ring up Mr Menzies and not to say anything about it to Miss Hurst. Well, I tried twice but the number was engaged and I had my dinner to think of, and when I did get through Miss Hurst came in and overheard. Not my fault,' defended Wotton vigorously, 'and I dare say it didn't make any difference really.'

'Anything else?'

'I warned her not to go saying anything to Miss Carter so she said she wouldn't. I went off about three, Barbara Hurst left a bit before that and said she'd be back before Mr Ralph went, so Miss Carter wouldn't be alone. I don't get back till late on my Sisterhood nights. She took the prescription with her, seemed quite upset she'd missed the doctor—proper gone on him she was, and no shame neither, and that's all I know. I didn't see Miss Carter when I came in, though Miss Hurst was still up. Just come out of the bathroom she had, and goodness knows what she puts in the water. Coal tar was good enough for us.'

'Now—think very carefully, Miss Wotton. Did she say anything to you about the tablets being missing and her having to ring up for a fresh supply?'

''Not a word,' said Wotton firmly.

'You're dead sure?'

'A body wouldn't be likely to forget a thing like that, seeing what followed.'

'I suppose not. Did you have much conversation with Miss Hurst?'

'I did not. At 11 o'clock of an evening I'm ripe for my bed. Ten's my proper time.'

'Don't the Sisterhood meetings generally go on so late?'

'They do not. But there was a new Sister there and I was told off to make her feel at home. Not that there was any necessity. That woman was like a geyser, thought I'd never get the tap turned off. No, to tell you the truth, I'd had enough chattering for one night, so I just said 'Good night' to Miss Hurst and off I went. I'm not one of these ladies that can lie in in the morning.'

'And the next thing you knew was finding Miss Carter dead in her bed when you took in the tea next day?'

'That's right. I got Miss Hurst to ring up Dr Crane but he was out, so presently we got my doctor and he came round at once. And that's all I can tell you.'

'Well, not quite all,' said Crook. 'There's the matter of the tablets. You do recognise that everything turns on them. Now— was there anything particular about this phial, in its appearance, I mean? Was it blue or red or . . . ?'

'Well, of course it wasn't,' said Wotton, 'it was just an ordinary phial.'

'I see. When did you last set eyes on it?'

'I wouldn't like to say. It was nothing to do with me. I was the housekeeper, Miss Hurst handled all the medicines.'

'Did you happen to notice if they were in the room that morning?'

'I didn't do Miss Carter's room; she liked Miss Hurst to do it.'

Crook tried again from another angle. 'Miss Carter had these tablets every night?'

'Every night. She couldn't sleep without them.'

'So she'd have had them the night before? You can be certain of that?'

'Quite certain.'

'And if the tablets had come to an end Miss Hurst would have ordered some more?'

'They hadn't come to an end. They were both asked that at the inquest, and they both said there should have been enough. Miss Hurst said the phial must have got thrown away with the rubbish—it was all piled up on the lift when she came back and she didn't dream of looking through it. . . .'

'Probably didn't think of it at the time. Well, it was either that or someone removed them. Tell me, did Miss Carter have any other medicine?'

'She was wicked over medicine. Bottle after bottle she'd pour down the basin, I've seen her myself. Think of all the sick folk who'd be grateful for that, I'd say to her, and they're welcome, she'd say back.'

'I didn't mean bottles, I meant tablets—headache pills, digestive pills, anything that might look like the sleeping-pills?'

'She had tablets for heartburn, but you couldn't mistake the two.'

'*You* couldn't, I dare say, but suppose you were a stranger, just coming in casually, and you saw some tablets in a tube on the dressing-table—would you know which they were—without picking them up or being told?'

'What the gentleman means,' put in Jessie helpfully, 'is do you think Mr Ralph could have seen the heartburn tablets and thought they were the sleeping-pills? It is an idea, Em.'

'Oh, Mr Crook's full of ideas, I don't doubt that. And not being an imbecile, Jessie, I know just what he's talking about. All I can say is if he didn't see the sleeping-tablets, *what became of them?*'

'When I know the answer to that one, Boadicea, the case 'ull be closed,' Crook assured her. 'Where were the tablets kept?'

'On the table beside the bed, with her books and a glass of water—you know.'

'And at the inquest no one seems to have suggested Ralph Carter might have seen the wrong tablets.'

'He said he saw the sleeping-pills. Very definite he was.'

'He's not so definite now, believe me.'

'Anyway, if they weren't there when he came, *who poisoned Miss Carter?* And there's no need to look in my direction. I didn't stand to gain anything, even if she'd have taken a dose from me, which she never did.'

The words went on ringing in Crook's ears after he had left Dunromin and was bowling back to London in the Old Superb. Was it an odd thing to say? And unless you're a lunatic you don't commit murder without a motive. He had discarded the notion that Miss Carter's death had been accidental. Someone had meant her to die, and had meant her to die before Menzies came the next morning. Crook knew all about the green-eyed monster, and, being remarkably well up in cases of actual crime, he knew that murder has been committed with no hope of personal gain but simply for revenge. The old story of the confidential maid displaced in the employer's mind by a newcomer was almost as old as the story of Adam and Eve. And indeed Adam and Eve weren't so irrelevant to the case as you might suppose. Cain had killed Abel because his offering had been preferred by Jehovah. Could Wotton be involved? He had no proof of that, but a good lawyer doesn't drop a good idea on that account. He scratches round as busy as a hen till he finds what he's looking for, and if it isn't there, well, he has to manufacture it. The police don't need a motive even for murder, though they're the first to admit that it does help. Men like Arthur Crook know that motive is the foundation of a murder case. So—motive there must be. In his own flat he never tried to cook anything more ambitious than a pair of kippers, but there wasn't a member of the Law List to beat him when it came to cooking of a subtler kind.

He might have been interested to hear Wotton's comment after his departure.

'He's going to try and put this on me,' she said. 'He'd stand by and see me hanged and never turn one of those vulgar red hairs of his.'

It wasn't everyone who read Crook so accurately at a first encounter.

Bill Parsons, Crook's right-hand man (I don't know where I'd be without Bill, he used to confess handsomely) was waiting in Bloomsbury Street when Crook returned.

'Anything come up about our Mr Carter?' Crook inquired.

'It's all according to Cocker.' Bill sounded pessimistic. 'He served in the Army Pay Corps in the First World War, rose to Major without ever hearing a shot fired; he used his title for a bit after the Armistice, but seems to have dropped it when he found that non-combatant service didn't cut much ice. He had a civilian job with a firm of grain merchants—never got far but paid in on a pension scheme—married the present Mrs Carter about 15 years ago. There had been a wife before that, but she blew off with a real soldier in 1917.'

135

'Don't blame her,' said Crook. 'Seen his marriage certificate?'

'For this one? Oh yes, Somerset House has the record. He's described as a widower.'

'Could be he was too optimistic. All the same, it wouldn't make any difference so far as the money's concerned. So long as he really is the chap he claims to be, he gets that anyway. Of course,' he added more cheerfully, 'he may have committed bigamy and someone told the old lady and he didn't want it to go any further. That's quite an idea. Can't trace the first wife, I suppose?'

'Seems to have gone off with a Canadian. No record of a divorce, and he waited long enough to marry again.'

'Not likely he'd want to risk a prison sentence for the present Mrs Carter,' Crook acknowledged. 'Beats me why the law sends men to jug for bigamy, as if they hadn't put themselves in prison as it was. Still, it wasn't me that made the laws under which we writhe. If it was, they'd be a lot more sensible than they are.'

'And you wouldn't be paying surtax,' suggested Bill.

Crook grinned unwillingly. 'Silver lining to every cloud,' he acknowledged. 'Too bad, though, that girl's lost her memory.' He explained the proceedings. 'I suppose for form's sake I shall have to have a word with the erstwhile lover, though if he's worth his salt he won't give her away, even if he knows anything.'

So off he went to get acquainted with Philip Crane, whom he found in what the Victorians would have called 'a state.' At first he was suspicious of Crook's intentions, cagey was Crook's own word.

'Come out of your hole,' Crook invited him. 'What are you afraid of?'

'Chaps like you,' said Philip candidly. 'No accusation was ever brought against Miss Hurst in connection with Miss Carter. In a word, this wasn't a police case. I don't want it to become one.'

'Meaning you know something?'

'Meaning I'm not talking.'

'Maybe I didn't make my position clear,' Crook offered

sunnily. 'I'm working for your young woman, and she's had the sense to put her cards on the table, some of 'em at all events; she's forgotten where she hid the ace. Now she's got the idea that you think she told you—are you with me?—that in some way she polished off the old lady. It's the essence of my case that she did nothing of the kind. Now—think hard. Can you remember exactly what she said? Not just the impression it made on you, but the words themselves.'

Crane looked doubtful. 'I wouldn't like to answer that on oath. The shock of what she admitted staggered me. It was after the inquest and I went to see her. "Thank goodness you're all right," I said, or something like that. "How ghastly it's been for you." And she said, "You don't know how frightened I've been, because I gave her the stuff. I hadn't any choice."'

'Happen to explain what she meant by that?'

'She went on, "It's not as terrible as it seems, is it? She couldn't have lived long and she would go without pain." I said, "Be careful what you're saying. If anyone heard you they'd think you were admitting responsibility." She said. "But that's the point. I am. Only I couldn't help it." Then she said something about Miss Carter seeing her lawyer. I said, "Did she tell you?" and she said, "No I found out by chance." She—Barbara, I mean—said, "Why should she want to harm me? She always seemed to want to help us." I asked her if she really thought the visit Menzies didn't eventually pay must be to do with her, and she said, "Why else? Who else stands to lose anything?" I ought to add she'd been through a fearful lot, she was half out of her mind, and I don't think either Wotton or Ralph Carter pretended to believe her story. I suppose I ought to have tried to get her out of the house, but the fact is she had nowhere to go, no relatives, not much money. . . . And then, after the funeral, when I came along to the house I was met by Wotton who said she'd disappeared. For a brief awful time I thought she might have put an end to things. I never thought of the fact.'

'That she might have lost her memory?'

'Poor darling, it's not really surprising. She had so much on her mind she had to get out somehow, and this was Nature's way.'

'Taking one consideration with another,' was Crook's dry comment, 'it's just as well you ain't giving evidence in a court of law. They don't have your respect for Nature's ways.'

Crane pushed his hands into his pockets and began to walk up and down the room with a stalking step, rather like his namesake.

'That old woman,' he burst out suddenly. 'She knew how to consume her own smoke. Never breathed a word about lawyers or Barbara or anything that last morning, only looking back and being wise after the event, which is the easiest parlour game I know, she didn't seem quite like herself. She told me the nephew was coming in and I knew there was no love lost there, and I thought he probably accounted for her slight agitation. I suppose . . .' he hesitated. 'This is the wildest of shots in the dark, but I suppose Wotton couldn't possibly know more than she's told?'

'I should say it was perfectly possible,' Crook assured him. 'Your old lady may have come right off a sugar cake, but there's no getting away from the fact she gave the old girl a pretty dirty deal.'

'But why take it out on Barbara?'

'Why does a man in a rage with his wife kick the cat? Besides, she may have believed in undue influence. All the same, you'll not bring a charge against Wotton in a hundred years. Your young lady,' he added, placidly, 'seems to evoke the little green-eyed god. The same situation seems to have cropped up at Preston.'

'Have you been down there?' inquired Crane.

Crook looked surprised. 'I'm not being asked to show that Miss Hurst had nothing to do with Mrs Calmady's death.'

'Can you separate the two?'

'My dear chap, you stick to medicine and leave the law to me,' Crook advised him. 'Do you suppose, if I could get the Archangel Gabriel to testify that her record was as clean as a whistle where Mrs Calmady was concerned, it would cut any ice in the Carter case? All the same, never leave a stone unturned, you might find something under it that 'ud be useful to sting the other chap—I don't seem to be getting much forrader this end, I might as well try Preston. Not,' he added frankly, as he bade his host farewell, 'that I think it'll get me very far.'

At first base, it got him no farther than the hall. Julie came whirling out of the drawing-room, like an animated snowflake, and listened contemptuously while he explained what she called his business.

'You can't really mean that this girl is such a fool she's contemplating more limelight?' she cried. 'Imagine the headline in the Press. BARBARA HURST. IS SHE A HOODOO? STRANGE STORY OF DOUBLE DEATH. Well, Mr Crook, I can assure you I'm perfectly prepared to meet her in court, if that's her idea.'

Crook didn't doubt it; she'd have faced her adversary on the edge of the Pit itself, in the hope of pushing the unfortunate creature into the lake of fire and brimstone that burneth for ever.

'Maybe we should go into your boodwar,' suggested Crook. 'You know what they say about walls having ears.'

She really was daffy, he realised, because she sidled up to the wall and cupping her hands, she whispered, 'Do you hear me? Barbara Hurst murdered my mother as well as Miss Carter.'

'Not there yourself by any chance?' suggested Crook, hustling her smartly into the drawing-room.

'I was down here talking to Mr Menzies. Miles, my cousin, was with us.'

'So Miss Hurst was the only person upstairs at the time—except your mother, of course?'

'That's right.'

'And how long had your mother been alone, Miss Calmady?'

'Two or three minutes, I dare say. What are you trying to do, Mr Crook? Whitewash Barbara Hurst?'

'Just get a few things straight,' said Crook. 'Always best to come to the fountain-head. Now, would two or three minutes be time enough for your mamma to have one of her fits—before Barbara Hurst went into the room, I mean?'

'The word is attack, not fits. My mother wasn't a dog.'

Well, that might be true, reflected Crook, but she'd given birth to as crazy a bitch as ever he hoped to encounter.

'Well, was there?' he persisted patiently.

139

'No. And I'll tell you why. Because, on my way down, I opened the door of her room and looked in to say, "I'll send Barbara up the minute she comes back," and she was perfectly composed then.'

'And yet when the young lady goes in a few minutes later it's like the universe before the Spirit breathed on Chaos.'

'That's her story. Naturally, I don't believe a word of it. It's obvious, she engineered a scene, not meaning my mother to have a chance of rescinding her will.'

'Come to that,' offered Crook, 'we don't know your lady mother would have changed it.'

'Not change it, when she knew who the girl really was? With one murder of an old woman to her credit. . . .'

'According to my clients, and they never lie (Ananias himself had been struck down for less than this) she intended to make a clean breast of the whole situation.'

'A bit late in the day,' sneered Julie.

'It was her first chance,' Crook protested. 'Till then, she didn't know. . . .'

'That's her story. Of course, she went straight upstairs to my mother. . . .'

'She must have stopped somewhere to drop a hat and a coat. Or was she wearing 'em when you came up?'

'Mere splitting of hairs,' crowed Julie. 'Her room was next door. It wouldn't take a moment to sling the things on the bed. And I must say she looked as though she'd been pulled through a hedge backwards. That girl had never taken time off to brush her hair or make herself presentable.'

'Know something?' said Crook pacifically. 'It's lucky for you you were born in this day and age. Think what a time you'd have had in the days of the scold's bridle. Lady, would you have been mad?'

He thought she was going to have a fit then and there. When she had calmed down a little, she said it was a clear waste of time talking to someone who had no right to be on the Law List anyway. Anyone less prejudiced would realise that no one but Barbara could have pushed the bell beyond the old woman's reach.

'Mightn't she have put out her hand and made a boss shot and pushed it out of reach herself?' Crook offered.

'Why should she?'

'Well, feeling for the tube of tablets.'

'She wouldn't. She'd have rung. Anyway, she'd never done that before.'

'There has to be a first time for everything. After all, people don't generally die more than once; once is enough to take the wrong dose or walk under a bus or fall in the fire. And she must have been a bit tired, having Menzies and all. No, Miss Calmady, I see how it is. You somehow never took to the girl, but all the same I don't see how you're going to make Barbara Hurst wear it, not if you try ever so.'

Julie saw him out. 'If you should think of coming again,' she said insolently, 'you might try the back door.'

'Thanks a million,' returned Crook gratefully. He doffed his appalling cap with a gesture that all but said: Will you kindly put a shilling in my little tambourine?—and jumped into that stately anachronism, the Old Superb, brave as spring in her yellow coat. He bowled rapidly round the corner, came back in reverse with the skill and speed of a trick cyclist, parked the car just out of the sight of the drawing-room windows, and walked round to the back door.

Florrie was like Em's sister, Jessie; she had a kind word for everyone.

'What is it to-day?' she asked. 'They don't buy nothing here. If there was any children, which there aren't, they'd be expected to grow feathers to keep themselves warm.'

Crook mightn't be acceptable to haughty maidens like Julie Calmady, but you couldn't fault him when it came to Florries and Jessies. In a space of about two minutes he was being offered a cup of tea as red as his suit. When he felt sure of his ground he introduced Barbara's name. Florrie's big silly eyes flew open.

'Fancy you knowing 'er! Shame Mrs Luke's not 'ere.'

"Oo's—I mean, who's Mrs Luke?'

Florrie explained. 'I could 'ave 'er along in two ticks,' she offered wistfully.

'What's two ticks?' asked the gallant Mr Crook.

So in about three ticks there they were, all sitting round the kitchen table, with their heads together, looking rather more ominous than Macbeth's three witches and a lot less glamorous.

'I never did believe she did the old lady any harm,' offered Flo.

'Bless your kind heart,' said Crook.

'Mind you,' put in Mrs Luke, as one not accustomed to being overlooked, 'she had something on her mind that last afternoon. I saw her after she came back—she was out when the lawyer fellow arrived.'

'When you say you saw her,' asked Crook carefully, 'do you mean when she came in from the street or after she came out of the drawing-room?'

'I was upstairs putting some of the things in the airing-cupboard, and she came up the stairs. Came up like a fairy as a rule, but—well, this fairy had been walking in treacle. Draggled she looked and no mistake, and not raining nor nothing. If she'd bin a different kind of a girl I'd have said she was in trouble—see?—that drawn look.' She cocked her head inquiringly. Crook said in impassive tones he wasn't a family man. 'The girls won't look at me,' he apologised.

'Marry a blind woman,' suggested Mrs Luke, with a loud laugh. 'Well, as I say, I saw her go into her room to take off her hat and I did wonder should I offer to bring her up a cuppa—Flo has the kettle on the hob all day—and then I thought, well, they'll be having their dinner any minute now. But I was proper worried, and I was just going to knock to see if she was all right when I saw the knob of the door turn, so I knew she'd be coming and I made myself scarce. Don't want anyone suggesting I'm a snooper. And I hadn't no more than got to the kitchen when the bell started ringing and all the fun begun. It was no wonder she looked like a ghost.'

He agreed that it wasn't, accepted another cup of tea (the things I do for Justice, he reflected, swallowing it as gallantly as if it had been beer) and oiled off in his fantastic Rolls, followed by their good wishes and hearty invitations to come down again any time he felt like it. His unchivalrous reflection as he drove townwards was that women were rather like serpents, without their tongues they weren't any good at all.

That, you might say, was the end of the evidence for the defence, and if only he'd had to clear Barbara of suspicion where old Mrs Calmady was concerned, he'd have been on velvet. But Miss Carter was quite a different cup of tea. That night at No 2 Brandon Street, Crook walked up and down, up and down with the regularity of a soldier on sentry-go. He had had the forethought to put on carpet slippers, so as not to ruin the night's rest of the tenant in the flat below, and as the hands moved round the clock the number of empty beer bottles increased.

'Something happened that last morning at the old lady's house that upset the apple-cart,' he insisted. 'Since no one telephoned and no one called except the doctor, the trouble must have come through the post. We know there were two letters, a prescription, a bill and an advertisement. The letters were from Ralph Carter, saying he was coming and bringing his documents with him, and old Pussy. No leads there. Then—how about Wotton? Could she have had a letter she suppressed? Or the girl herself? But no! Wotton took in the post; if there'd been one addressed to Barbara Hurst we should have heard about it before this. Or—did Miss Carter say something to the girl that she doesn't remember? Nuts. In a household like that Wotton would go round with her ears on sticks; she's like Mrs Luke, they don't miss much. So if she didn't hear anything and she didn't leave the flat till after Ralph Carter arrived, odds are there wasn't anything to hear. And yet—out of the blue Miss Carter wants to see her lawyer, and she don't want Barbara Hurst to know he's been sent for. But (it was like walking up a spiral staircase, you could never be sure what 'ud meet your eye at the next turn) Miss Hurst found out. Well then, did she tackle the old lady when she had her to herself? Did she really know why Menzies was coming over? And how much difference was it going to make to her? And then the old woman's remark to Wotton about being deceived and experience not being worth anything unless you profited from it. It all ties up somewhere, but how?'

Up and down he prowled. Try as he might he couldn't link Wotton with the death. She didn't stand to gain enough—just fifty pounds and some junky old furniture. Ralph then? But how can you be deceived in someone you've mistrusted from the word Go? So it was: Here we go round the mulberry-bush, the mulberry-bush, the mulberry-bush, and every time the music stopped it was Barbara who was odd man out. Which in the nature of things was impossible.

Later he was to wonder how he'd missed such an obvious clue, but for the moment he was flummoxed. It was 48 hours before light dawned in that jungly brain, and 'I knew it was the letters,' he told Bill. 'Wonder what the original enclosure was.'

CHAPTER 11

After Crook had gone, Julie went up to her room and sat staring out of the window, staring at nothing. It never occurred to her that Crook might constitute a danger. A rough common man, she thought; it wasn't likely a court of law would pay any attention to him. The day, that had been bright enough, was now clouding over; a mist rose from the sea, pushing steadfastly, doggedly over the beach and the parade, moving towards the house. It didn't affect her in the sense that it would prevent her going out, since she had no reason either for going or coming. She felt as though Life, that had always been her enemy, had hit her over the head with a brickbat; she was immobilised. Her existence had always been bitter as aloes, now it was suffocating as churchyard dust. One day, she used to comfort herself, I shall have a life of my own, no duties, no ties, and she would dream of what she would do with liberty when it was hers. And now the hour had struck and the new life was no more than an empty sack, and there was nothing to put into it.

With old Mrs Calmady in the churchyard, Miles more than ever occupied with his own affairs and the girl, Barbara, gone for good, the house was as quiet as a grave, as quiet and as cold.

Miles tried to rouse her. 'Menzies wants to know what you intend to do about the house,' he said.

'When I've made up my mind I'll let him know.'

'He's got a client who he thinks would make you a substantial offer.'

'And in the meantime where am I supposed to sleep? It's nothing to him that I should be turned out of my house at short notice to suit his precious client's convenience.'

145

'But you can't mean to stay here. It's far too large.'

'We can shut some of the rooms.'

'I shan't be here permanently.'

'Rats leaving the sinking ship.'

'My dear Julie, you know that's a ridiculous simile. I stayed on to please your mother, but it was always agreed that when I wanted to make a home of my own . . .'

'You'll need a housekeeper, won't you?'

He said gently, 'Julie, you must appreciate that one of these days I shall want to get married.'

Fire had leapt into her eyes. 'Not that girl. Not Mother's murderer.'

'You'll find yourself in Queer Street if you go round saying things like that,' he warned her. 'There's such a thing as a law of slander. . . .'

'And you think that girl's going to take me to court? You must be out of your mind. She's only too grateful she's not been taken there herself, and she may be yet.'

'Whom I marry and when and where I live is no longer any concern of yours, Julie. If Barbara will have me . . .'

She began to laugh. 'I always knew it was a plot. Well, I should congratulate you, perhaps, that you've pulled it off. Don't give a thought to my future, will you?'

'You know perfectly well your future matters a good deal to me. You're . . .' he paused.

'Mother's legacy,' she taunted him. 'Her only one. Still Barbara has her five thousand pounds, and of course there's the legacy from Miss Carter. She's a clever girl, isn't she, Miles? You ought never to be too hard up.'

He said abruptly, 'Julie, you're ill. You should see Stuart.'

'Stuart? That blind old fool. He couldn't even see Mother had been murdered. . . .'

To all his suggestions she raised some adverse criticism. 'Why not get a small house in the neighbourhood?' he said. 'You must have friends here after twenty years.'

'I've no friends,' she said fiercely, 'and you know it.'

'Then London. A flat. You'll be quite well off. And there's always something going on in London.'

'Picture galleries. And concerts. And cinemas. Always alone. And then a nice cup of tea and a buttered bun at a café, wondering if the woman who shares my table will make the first move. Or making a fourth where all the other three are friends and knowing they're dying for you to go. And when that palls I can take the bus home to my spotless little flat, spotless because there's no one to make a mess of it, and cook myself such an amusing little meal in my kitchenette, wearing one of these dressy nylon aprons, like an American hostess. And of course there's always, in London, television. Oh, Miles, how anxious you are to shuffle off your responsibility.'

He had frowned. 'Is responsibility quite the word?'

'Certainly. I've spent all my life looking after Mother. Now someone owes me something.'

'You talk as if you were an old woman, Julie,' he protested. 'You're the right side of 50. These days that's no age at all. It's certainly not too late to cultivate new interests. . . .'

'Church work?' asked Julie, sending him a fiendish look. 'Offering to help clean the altar brass and find that newcomers only get the font ewer. Well, I'm not going to be fobbed off with the font ewer for the rest of my days.'

'There's voluntary work,' he suggested, but the persuasive note in his voice was now overlaid with anxiety. What he wanted, quite selfishly, was to get Julie out of the district. She admitted she had no friends, and obviously she had no happy memories. And if and when he, Miles, brought Barbara back here as his wife, it would cause a lot less complication if Julie were, say, a hundred miles away.

Julie laughed. 'I've done enough work in my time,' she declared. 'Now I want a little stimulus.'

He was more anxious about her than he cared to show. He knew she was making wild accusations against Barbara Hurst; he couldn't help noticing, when he dropped into the Cat and Chickens or the Lady and Lamb, how eyes slewed round in his direction. As he correctly surmised, he had Mrs Luke to thank for all this covert publicity. She was having a whale of a time, with Rumour for company. She took him from the Cat to the Lady, and even as far as the Blackbird in Beachampton, and every time she exhibited him he was a bit more furbished up. That is, at the Cat he was almost as naked as Cupid, but by the time he'd run the gamut, via the Wheatsheaf, the Live and Let Live and the Case is Altered, he could practically have set out for an Eskimo holiday on the spot. Many a glass of stout laced with you-know-what was the chatty Mrs Luke offered as a kind of entertainment tax. Openly she deplored Flo's lack of initiative.

'The chances that girl has,' she would mourn. 'As I tell her, what's a bit of earache in exchange for what she could pick up if she'd put her mind to it?'

On the day of Crook's visit Miles, with a friend, stopped at the Lady for a pint on the way home. Mrs Luke was there, and from the way she was talking, the low rapt voice, the ducked head, the enthralled circle about her, he decided, sensitively, that something fresh had turned up at the house. He never used to have these sensitive intuitions, as he supposed a woman would call them; and more than ever was he resolved to hunt Julie away, as you'd hunt a witch. The trouble was, he reflected, when he had parted from his companion and was walking home, she had no friends and had lost any capacity she might once have had to attract them. He saw her a few years ahead, one of those queer old women, women who age before their time, scurrying up and down the street, head bent, lips working perpetually, living in a kind of nightmare world of frustration and defiance. It wasn't a pretty picture. He shuddered.

When he went into the drawing-room there was no one there. Miss Julie was in her room, Florrie said. The gentleman that came this afternoon seemed to have upset her.

'Who was that?' murmured Miles.

'A gentleman from London. It was about Miss Hurst.'

'Miss Hurst?' His whole being stiffened. 'Why, nothing's happened, has it?'

Hearing voices, Julie came hurrying in. 'You're very late, Miles. Can I take it that you're in touch with Barbara Hurst?'

He looked a little surprised. 'I haven't seen her since she left Preston, but naturally I hear through Menzies, who's keeping in touch.'

'I don't know if we've got Mr Menzies to thank for that vulgarian who called this afternoon, but *I will not receive such creatures in my house*. Is that clear?'

'Calm down,' he implored her. 'Who is this monstrosity?'

'His name's Crook.'

'Crook?'

'Crook. I must admit that seems much more apposite. Anyway, he came here talking about actions and rights and I don't know what nonsense. As if that girl had the smallest intention of taking her case to court, assuming she has a case, which I don't allow. Why, she hasn't a leg to stand on.'

'I suppose,' said Miles thoughtfully, 'that's what Mrs Luke was discussing at the Lady and Lamb to-night.'

She cried disdainfully, 'So that's where you've been.'

'That's where I've been,' he agreed. 'Candidly, Julie, you must put a bridle on your tongue, or you'll find yourself in serious trouble. And I've had another letter from Menzies,' he went on, 'asking about the house. This substantial client . . .'

'I'm not going to be hounded out of my own house,' flared Julie.

He shrugged. 'Please yourself. I'm going up to see him the day after to-morrow, there are various points to settle.'

'Including my future, I suppose? When will you get it into your head that I'm not a piece of merchandise to be disposed of? I have my own life, and I propose to shape it in my own way.'

Later that evening she said she might come to London with him. 'I don't want you two hatching plots behind my back.'

There was no doubt about it, he reflected, as he prepared for bed, she'd gone a deal queerer since her mother's death. It was as if, for all her bitter complaints, Mrs Calmady had been the kingpin of her existence; withdraw that and the whole structure fell into ruins.

He watched her that evening as she sat by the fire, twisting her hands together, noticed the strength of those thin, writhing fingers, the strained knuckles, the bony wrists, and he knew a real spasm of horror at the thought of Barbara Hurst in this mad woman's power.

The following evening she told him she had decided to come to London the next day, and they agreed to travel up on the convenient 10.4 that stopped only at Beachampton and St. Hillary. Miles hoped, sheepishly, to be able to pass the buck to the lawyer. It was tough on him, perhaps, and much fairer if Cutbush had been in the office to accept responsibility, but Cutbush was down with pleurisy and would need convalescence before he was back in harness, and so the burden would fall on Menzies's shoulders. Still, reflected Miles, that's what the chap was paid for, and he could fix his own terms.

The Friday morning dawned bright, if chill, and Miles came down with a sense of relief. Soon now he could leave this Nightmare Abbey of a house and start making plans of his own. True, he hadn't asked Barbara to marry him and there was a possibility that, while the shadow of Miss Carter's death hung over her head, she'd stall him. And, of course, there was that fellow, Crane. But he didn't rate him very high. By all accounts, the engagement had been broken off before Barbara Hurst became Barbara Field. True, it was an invidious position for the young doctor, with Wotton fulfilling in that household much the position of Mrs Luke at Preston, and telling all and sundry that most likely it was a put-up job between them, but now if ever the girl needed support.

'If she was in love with him she wouldn't have broken it off,' he decided. 'If, on the other hand, it was he who put the kybosh on things, then he's no husband for her.'

If he could shake Julie off he might go round to Linton Mansions and see her for himself. He had never given Julie the address, and he must have a quick word with Menzies, warning him not to supply it. Barbara had had enough to put up with without an unheralded call from her worst enemy.

Things didn't work out in the least as he had anticipated. When he came down to breakfast there was no sign of Julie. The meal progressed to the marmalade stage and Florrie came in with a fresh rack of toast, and still his cousin hadn't appeared.

'Is Miss Calmady breakfasting in bed?' he asked cheerfully, his countenance bright with anticipation of ridding himself of Julie in the near future.

Florrie goggled. 'Miss Julie? She went to London on the early train. Didn't take any more than a cup of tea either. Said she could get something on the way.'

She saw the tightening of his mouth and the wary look that jumped into his eyes, though all he said was, 'She must have changed her mind, I suppose.'

Florrie scurried off; here would be something to tell Mrs Luke when she came this afternoon.

Miles travelled up to town with a premonition of disaster dogging him all the way. At first he had thought Julie's stealing a march on him a typically childish gesture. She wasn't going to be treated like a piece of merchandise, she said, and she meant to get the first word with the lawyer. That's what he thought to start with; but as he neared London another thought struck him, and he wished he'd had the good sense to telephone Menzies from Preston, warning him that Julie might be coming in and might possibly ask for Barbara's address. When the train reached London he thrust his way off the platform, snapped up a taxi and was driven at once to Menzies's office. Here he had to wait a few minutes, fuming and fussing in a manner very unlike his normal demeanour. As soon as he was with the lawyer he said, 'Has my cousin been here this morning?'

'Yes,' agreed Menzies, 'she told me you would be coming along later. Well, naturally I knew that, since we had the appointment.'

'Did she say what she wanted?'

Menzies thought the fellow looked remarkably agitated. 'She apparently found a list among her mother's papers of certain pieces of jewellery she wanted Miss Hurst to have, and she thought she'd hand them over in person. What's wrong?' he added sharply.

'Do you mean to say you fell for that?' exclaimed Miles.

'I don't understand you.'

'It was just a trick to get Barbara's address. There was no such list, and if there had been Julie wouldn't have honoured it.'

'She can't do her any harm,' said Menzies uneasily..

'That's all you know. Didn't she strike you as being as crazy as a coot? I tell you, she's mulled over this till she probably really does believe Barbara murdered Mrs Calmady.'

Menzies picked up the telephone. 'I'll ring through to Barbara, see if your cousin's there or has been and gone or what.'

But though both men could hear the bell ringing there was no reply.

'I'm going round,' said Miles, that premonition of irreparable disaster still riding him like a nightmare.

'If she doesn't answer the telephone the odds are she isn't there,' Menzies pointed out, reasonably. 'Your cousin either didn't find her at home or they've finished their conversation and both gone out.'

'To have a cup of coffee over the road, I suppose.' Miles's voice was bitter in its irony.

'She may have gone to see Crook or anything.'

'Crook? That's the chap who put the wind up Julie. Why on earth should Barbara be there?'

'I don't know,' confessed Menzies, who was dialling Crook's number. 'But there's never any harm keeping in touch with him.'

He had to dial twice before he could get his connection. 'Barbara Hurst here?' exploded Crook. 'Why on earth should she be? What's that? You gave Miss Calmady the address? I hope you'll enjoy seeing your picture in the paper as accessory before the fact. On my Sam, Menzies, you should have your head examined. That woman's already committed one murder and *ce n'est que le premier pas qui coûte.*' His accent would have made a famous statesman sound like a native of Paris. 'Don't hold me up,' he went on peremptorily, as Menzies tried to get a word in edgeways, 'I'm on my way.'

Menzies slung down the receiver, rushed at a peg and took down a soft dark hat.

'Coming?' he inquired of the startled Miles. 'According to Crook, your cousin's already got one corpse to her credit, and so far as I'm concerned once is once too often.'

Since her return to London Barbara had lived a life of the

utmost seclusion. She felt like someone not completely attuned to any one atmosphere, she might float or sink or even dissolve. She knew that she was Barbara Hurst but the name had no more connection with herself as a person than Barbara Field or Barbara Fitton. Some wayward fate had cut the string that tethered her to the normal world, and she alternately bobbed and fell with no sense of security anywhere. She looked at the photographs of lost girls in the Sunday papers and could even envy them. They were lost only in the sense that their relations didn't know where they were, but they themselves knew. It seemed to her that she was less fortunate still, because though she knew Barbara Hurst's address and outstared her day by day in the oval looking-glass on her dressing-table, she still didn't know who Barbara Hurst was.

Since her excursions into the past, in the hope of recovering her individuality—and what stimulus *they* had lent to the days—she had spent the time in the flat or going to the cinema. She dared not look for work at the moment, and her own future seemed as precarious as that of Humpty-Dumpty. At any instant, she felt, she might fall off her wall, and then no one would be able to put her together again.

'Wait for it, sugar,' Crook would encourage her. 'Trust your Uncle Arthur, the man who put the T in truth.'

When she heard the bell on this Friday morning Barbara supposed it was Crook outside. Who else was likely to call, unless it was a boy with onions or someone wanting another flat? Thinking this, she opened the door and nearly fell backward in astonishment when she saw Julie standing there.

'I hope I'm not interrupting you when you're working,' said Julie, pushing past and staring about her. 'This is what they call a luxury flat, I suppose. Well, no doubt you can afford it now. Two four-figure legacies in a year must have changed your situation appreciably.'

'I've only got it for a short time,' said Barbara, carefully. 'Mr Menzies arranged it for me.'

'Just a *pied-à-terre* until your marriage, I dare say.'

'I'm not considering marrying anyone—at present.' Barbara's voice sharpened.

'You don't mean to tell me Miles has backed down? Oh, but you mustn't give up hope. He's only marking time, I'm certain, till you've really got the money.'

Barbara said abruptly, 'Why have you come?' to which Julie replied: 'To warn you that if you try to carry out your plot I shall accuse you of murder. It wouldn't look very well, even if you did manage to get a verdict, not twice in about six weeks, you know.'

'I've no idea what you're talking about,' said the girl, beginning to feel apprehensive. 'What plot?'

'Your plot with Miles. But I mean what I say.'

'If Miles asks me to marry him and I want to, you can't prevent it,' said Barbara, trying to maintain a calm stance. 'And if your mother were still alive she certainly wouldn't refuse— I'm sure she wouldn't. Why, she was fond of me, you know she was.'

'At first perhaps.' Julie's face was terrible to see. 'But not afterwards, not when she knew.'

'Knew what? That I wasn't Barbara Fitton? But—you were there yourself. She gave me the pearls, knowing I wasn't her granddaughter.'

'Ah, but she hadn't realised then that you'd sneaked into the house by a back door, so to speak. When she understood that, that it had all been a trick—oh, after that she didn't mean to let you play ducks and drakes with her money, laugh at her when she was out of the way. . . .'

'Stop! Stop!' Barbara put out a hand as if she were beating off a wedge of oppressive flies that threatened to suffocate her. 'You don't know what you're saying. She only realised who I was the day before she died. . . .'

'Oh no,' contradicted Julie, 'she didn't realise it then. She only knew you weren't Barbara Fitton, and you saw to it that she should never know you were really Barbara Hurst.'

'You're wrong,' said the girl. 'I realised she would have to know. Mr Menzies was going to tell you and you would come rushing up. I thought it would be better for her to hear it from me. I went into my room to get tidy, as you suggested, and I stayed there a few minutes thinking how to face this new situation, how to tell her without giving her too much of a shock. I didn't know then that the codicil had been signed; none of us did, you didn't yourself. Then I went in—and it was too late. She couldn't speak, couldn't hear. I don't think she even knew who I was. The rest you know.'

'How conveniently it all happened, assuming your story's the truth,' Julie taunted her. 'She amends her will, leaving you £5000, and just when she's going to hear what a climber and charlatan you are, she dies. How very, very simple.'

Barbara was shaking from head to foot. 'It is the truth,' she insisted. 'It's dreadful, it's all dreadful, but my one consolation is that she died believing in me. I couldn't have borne to shake her faith, though somehow I think she would have believed me, if she had known.'

'Liar!' The word broke with the violence of a stone skimming through a glass window. 'She did know, and she didn't believe.'

'How could she know? Mr Menzies had only just told us. There hadn't been time . . .'

'I don't mean about Barbara Hurst. I mean about you and Miles, and the furtive complicated plan you evolved between you. Oh, you're a clever actress, Barbara Hurst, but she knew about you in the end.'

'That's absurd.' Barbara struggled to keep her voice calm. 'If she had really believed I was cheating her, plotting with her own nephew, would she have sent for Mr Menzies and changed her will?'

'Ah, but she didn't know then—it was afterwards. And she was going to change it—make no mistake about that. And she warned you she was going to change it, and in telling you that she signed her death warrant. You didn't mean her to have the opportunity. . . . What is it?' Her voice changed abruptly. 'Why are you looking at me like that? With murder in mind?'

'It can't be true,' said Barbara. 'Even you wouldn't do that.'

'Even I?'

'Yes. Because, after she signed the codicil, nobody saw her except you, so who could have told her about Miles and me—except you? Did you, Julie? Did you? In the hope of persuading her to destroy the codicil? Or did you—did you mean her to have a heart attack, believing, as you did, that the signature hadn't been added?'

The words came faster and faster, falling over themselves. The world about them had lost its normal shape and substance; the air clouded with a blood-red haze and through that haze peered Julie's face, blown up like an enormous cloud.

'You did it,' repeated Barbara, 'because of the money. That's all. Because of the money. Like Judas and the thirty pieces of silver.' Someone was screeching, she didn't know who. Not Julie, because her mouth hung open, her eyes were wide and empty. It was like that day on the parade when suddenly someone began to laugh—and laugh. 'You went in and—what did you say? Enough to bring on one of her attacks. And then—and then—why didn't she ring the bell? Because you were there, because you could give her the drops. Then why did she upset them? Perhaps because you went away and left her—but she'd have rung the bell. Unless—unless—of course, it was you who moved the bell. You knew she was going to have an attack, so you went away and left her, having made sure she couldn't get anyone to help her. You're a murderess—your own mother! Why, it wouldn't even surprise me to know that you'd deliberately emptied the drops over the sheet. Did you? Did you?'

Julie's voice came screaming back. 'You're mad, everyone knows you're mad. Not that that'll save you. Try telling that story, just try it. Why, even your precious Dr Crane wouldn't believe it.'

'Dr Crane! Barbara turned, her wild glance fell on the telephone, she snatched the receiver from its rest. She dialled a number.

Philip Crane's voice at the other end of the line sounded so cool it was like rain falling through a zone of torrid heat.

'Philip, it's you. This is Barbara here. I know I shouldn't be ringing you during working hours, but oh believe me, none of your patients needs you more than I.'

'What on earth's happened? Have you had an accident?'

'No, no. I wouldn't disturb you for that. There are other

doctors, but—no one but you can help me now. Philip, I understand the truth at last.'

'The truth?'

'Yes. I mean—I know who killed her.'

'You mean, your memory's restored? You can think clearly again? Listen! Where are you speaking from?'

'I'm at the flat.'

'Alone?'

'No, no, Julie Calmady's here. She—she's mad, Philip, and I'm afraid. She's dangerous.'

The young doctor could hear the sound of Julie's hoarse laughter shuddering along the line.

'Can you get rid of her? If not, don't let her trap you. *Don't say anything at all.* Let her do the talking, if she wants to, but don't let her involve you in an argument. I'm coming, as quickly as I can. I shall regard it as an emergency. Now, Barbara, remember what I say. Watch out for yourself, and—I'm coming now.'

He rang off. Barbara turned, her white face strained but triumph in her voice.

'Did you hear that? He's coming.'

'About time we did have a doctor on the scene,' retorted Julie. 'I only hope he brings his strait-waistcoat with him. He'll certainly be able to use it.'

The girl remembered her lover's advice, and turned resolutely to the window. The sky had clouded over, not many people were about. Julie was still talking, but she closed her ears to the words. Don't listen, don't listen. The words throbbed in her brain. Think of something else. Ah, but what? She had an appalled feeling that all this had happened before, that she was like a traveller who takes an alleged short cut only to find himself going round in a circle and eventually intersecting the road at a point he hitherto passed on his journey. She was not escaping terror as she had hoped, she had merely returned to its kingdom. The disillusion, the tragedy, the fear were all hatefully familiar.

And I, like one lost in a thorny wood,
That rents the thorns, and is rent with the thorns,
Seeking a way, and straying from the way;
Not knowing how to find the open air,
But toiling desperately to find it out.

She had learned that long ago, at school presumably, when she was that unfortunate creature, an orphan evacuee. She repeated the words over and over; while behind her, like the pitiless booming of the sea, Julie's voice went on and on.

'Have you gone deaf as well as demented?' shouted Julie. 'If you knew how mad you look, standing there, mouthing nothings. Anyone would certify you on sight.'

She turned, her control breaking. 'I've nothing to say to you, you—you monster. To murder your own mother—for that's what it was, if you never laid a finger on her.'

'You're the expert,' jeered Julie. 'You should know.'

They were like two snakes hissing at one another from either side of one of those fussy little tables that are littered with souvenirs. It had a cloth of white satin embroidered with gold, with a deep purple satin hem. There was a design on the white satin of a man riding on a ritual elephant. She noticed it all impersonally, and all the while a bell seemed to be ringing in her ears; but she wouldn't listen, she wouldn't listen, and presently the telephone stopped. Julie didn't seem to have heard it either. One of the ornaments on the silly little table was a miniature dagger, a scimitar, she thought detachedly. Quite sharp it was; she knew because she had tried it one day when she was dusting. Now Julie's eyes were also upon it. It looked no larger than a toy, but—wasn't there a classic case of someone being stabbed with a bare bodkin? Then how much more deadly might even a miniature dagger be? Her hand shot out, met another hand, her voice said something scarcely comprehensible even to the speaker: Julie's big fingers caught hers and bent them back; she uttered a little cry. The table swayed and overturned; a lot of trash was spilt on the floor, but the little knife wasn't part of it. Next the telephone went over with a shrill ping of protest; a chair swayed and fell. And in the middle of the chaos the two women fought, silent now, like two of the deadly scorpions of the desert, struggling implacably and without pity to the bitter death.

Philip Crane made the journey from Ferriby Park to Linton Mansions in record time. He passed other cars on the wrong side, he overtook, he jumped the lights, he nearly did for himself by refusing to give way to a lorry at a crossroads; the lorry-driver's language was so inflammatory it was a wonder it didn't ignite his load, which was first-grade petrol, but Philip didn't hear him. Nervous drivers were edged into the pavement, and a lady with a conspicuous L on the front of her car told her instructor in shaken tones that she'd changed her mind and wouldn't bother about taking the Test after all; it wasn't going to be any pleasure driving with hogs like that running you down every day of the week. When he reached Linton Mansions he leaped out of the car and dashed into the hall. The porter was sitting in a grandfather chair, with a detective story open on a high club kerb round a handsome fire. He looked up with a slightly disapproving air as Philip dashed in.

But before he could ask if there was anything he could do his impetuous visitor had fled past him and was dragging back the lift gates. The porter came up at the double.

'What's all this?' he demanded indignantly. 'Can't you read?' He indicated a notice on the wall of the lift. 'No unauthorised person may work this lift. I'm the only authorised one round here.' He stepped inside and slammed the door. 'Which floor?'

'Miss Hurst.'

'Hurst? Oh, her that has Miss Merton's flat.' He pressed a button and the lift sailed upwards. 'Expecting you? She's got a lady with her—unless she left while I was having my elevenses.'

'I'm quite aware of that. That's why I'm here. I'm a doctor, I received an S O S.'

'Why ever couldn't you say so?'

He stopped the lift and opened the gates. 'Don't go,' said Philip. 'I may need you.'

He rang and knocked on the door of No 22 but no one heard him. He laid his ear against the crack.

'Here, you,' he called to the porter. 'Got a masterkey? Then bring it out.'

'I'm not supposed to use it, not when tenants are in their flats.'

'And if a tenant falls down and breaks her leg, I suppose she dies in misery because of your red tape. If you don't open the door right away I'll kick the damned thing down. Hasn't it occurred to you yet that this may be a case of murder?'

That shook the porter good and proper; he fumbled in his trouser-pocket, produced a key and opened the door as sharp as winking. Philip raced past him through the tiny lobby and into the living-room. The sight that met his eyes stayed him for a moment in pure horror. One of the women—that would be Julie Calmady, whom he'd never met—was lying crumpled against the wainscot, while bending over her with the face of a maniac, was Barbara Hurst, and in her hand that was uplifted as if to strike, gleamed the little Turkish dagger.

160

CHAPTER 12

The first instant of shock over, he was on her like a flash, had wrested the weapon from her hand.

'Barbara, what on earth . . . ? Have you taken leave of your senses? I warned you. . . .'

'You don't understand.' She was sobbing. 'She was going to attack me.'

'And you had the knife? Stay quietly there, I must see to her.'

He dropped on his knees beside the recumbent woman. 'She's breathing all right,' he said grimly. She didn't seem wounded either, not so much as a scratch. So Barbara's story might be true, she might indeed have wrested the knife from her adversary. 'What happened?' he went on, still not looking round.

'She came to see me, I didn't ask her, she was accusing me of murdering her mother, and it's not true, Philip, it's not true. She did it herself.'

'Murdered her own mother? Barbara, my dear girl. . . .'

'I know. I know. But she betrayed herself, and when she saw that she seemed to go out of her mind. She meant to stop Mrs Calmady signing the codicil, and this way it didn't seem to her she could ever be suspected.'

Philip stood up. 'Give me a hand,' he said. 'It's slight concussion probably caused by the fall. She must have hit her head. Nothing to worry about. We'll put her on the sofa.'

Barbara shook her head and retreated a few steps. 'I couldn't touch her—really, Philip.'

The young doctor might well be forgiven for supposing he'd

161

stepped into Colney Hatch, but before he could utter a further protest steps sounded in the corridor and the front door pealed as though someone intended to wake the dead.

The porter had been reluctantly recalled to his duties by a voice bawling up the lift shaft. He wanted to stay and see what was happening, but he didn't want any more complaints reaching the management. He wasn't as young as he had been and whatever they might say about full employment he knew he wouldn't be everybody's money. So sulkily he slammed the gates and took the lift downstairs. A woman tenant, known as Lady Himuckamuck, was waiting for him, staring at the empty grille out of a perfect woodland of little fur animals that writhed and contorted themselves round her scrawny throat. Seen through the bars of the lift she looked like some unattractive product out of a foreign zoo. She had a tongue as long as an anteater's and she played it on him during the mercifully brief journey to the first floor. She had larger feet than most, but it would never have occurred to her to use them to walk up one flight of stairs. And he'd only just clashed the gates to when he heard more feet in the hall and two men came rushing in as if the cops were after them. And for all he knew they were—so Hill thought, till he recognised one of the men as the lawyer chap who'd let what the impressionable Mr Hill now thought of as the Murder Flat.

They came haring through the hall, and 'Miss Hurst,' said the lawyer. He was just going to press the button when the other fellow caught his arm.

'Half a minute,' he said. 'Here's Crook.'

An absurd high yellow car had stopped outside the flats and the porter rubbed his eyes, believing for one astounded minute that Mr Magoo had jumped straight out of the screen and was prancing through the hall. He bounded up to the lift, as bouncy as a rubber ball, and squeezed his way in.

'When shall we three meet again?' he quoted. (He was a sucker for clichés.) 'Make it snappy, Joe. You wouldn't want to be accessory to a murder, would you?'

That made two of them talking about murder, thought Hill.

The directors weren't going to like this. They didn't think murder was nice, not nice at all.

'How many up there to date?' the bright brown Inconceivable continued.

'There's Miss Hurst, of course, and a lady and a doctor just come in. Telephoned for, I understood.'

'Three of them? H'm. There's been two corpses already in this case, and you know what they say about three being a crowd?'

Hill felt shaken; he decided he'd step down to his own doctor to-night and get a pick-me-up. He liked a quiet life, had seen all the violence he cared about in two world wars. He preferred his crime by proxy these days, like all sensible men.

'Stand by,' Crook warned him, just as the doctor had done. 'We may need you to let us in.'

But the door was opened almost at once by Barbara herself. She no longer held the knife, but one hand clapsed her other wrist; she seemed beyond speech, but Crane looking over his shoulder, said impatiently, 'One of you help me to lift Miss Calmady on to the sofa. There's nothing to worry about. She's only hit her head as she fell. No need for an ambulance, we don't want to tangle with the authorities at this stage. She'll come round of her own accord quite soon.'

'Nice for her to stay asleep a little while,' offered Crook, as Miles went to the doctor's assistance. 'One wild animal at a time is as much as I care to cope with, outside of the zoo, of course. Now then, sugar'—this to Barbara—'what gives?'

Gently he took her wrist in his immense hand; a trickle of blood was flowing.

'It's only a scratch,' explained Barbara. 'That must have been when I wrenched the knife away.'

'Trust a jane,' said Crook in resigned tones. 'Always in mischief if you take your eyes off them for a second.'

'She killed her mother,' said Barbara in a flat, colourless voice, 'and I'd just realised it.'

Miles turned from the sofa. 'What's that you said?'

'It was Julie. Honestly, I think she's mad. To do that to your own mother. It was bad enough before when I thought

she was alone, but to have your own daughter standing
by . . .'

'Be careful,' said Menzies. 'You're bringing a very grave
charge.'

'No graver than Miss Calmady brought against my client,'
said Crook, 'and we know that was all boloney. I've got a
witness. . . .'

'A witness?' They were all staring, but it was Barbara who
said, 'You can't have. I mean, she wouldn't have done *that* if
there'd been anyone else there; and we know where everyone
else was.'

'You've got me wrong, sugar,' explained Crook, patiently. 'I
don't mean I've got a witness that Miss Calmady did it, though
the inference as to her guilt is very strong. But that ain't my
pigeon. What I mean is that I've got a witness it couldn't have
been you.'

Even Julie was forgotten now; the eyes of all them were
on Crook's big red pug face.

'Mrs Luke saw you go upstairs and into your room, and you
stayed there so long she thought you might have had a fit or
something; she was just going to come in and ask if there was
anything she could do when you started comin' out, so she made
herself scarce. You went along to Mrs Calmady's room, and
by the time Luke had reached the kitchen the bell was ringin'
like mad. So, you see, even if you'd had the will to murder,
the opportunity was lacking.'

Miles said, 'I never did believe it was Barbara. But, Crook,
you say the inference against my cousin is very strong. Since
she's not yet come round this might be as good an opportunity
as any to explain that.'

'Plain as the nose on my face,' said Crook, shortly. 'Miss C.
says her Mamma was all right when she left her and the bell
was in place. Then, if she felt an attack coming on, *why didn't
she ring?* There's only one answer to that which was that the
bell was out of reach. No one had been in since Miss Calmady,
so—QED. You can't have it both ways—either the old lady
had started one of her attacks before her daughter came downstairs, in which case why didn't daughter give her the drops, or

it came on sudden when she was alone—in which case who moved the bell?'

'If it was quite unexpected and very acute . . .' Miles began, but Crook snapped him up like a cow plucking a daisy.

'Too acute to press a bell but not so acute she couldn't fumble for the phial and remove the cork? That cock won't fight, Calmady. No, that was her home-work.' He looked down at the unconscious woman on the couch and even his tough heart knew a stab of compassion. He always held that at least half the people that get themselves murdered have asked for it, and he didn't hold Mrs Calmady entirely guiltless. Julie, lying there witless and blank, made him think of a deserted waste land, a place where no one comes and no flowers grow.

He was startled at the thought. 'Wake up, Arthur,' he adjured himself, 'or you'll join the army behind bars.'

Miles was saying in staggered tones, 'Are you really suggesting that Julie would do that for a wretched five thousand pounds?'

'Oh, I'd say the money was only a symbol,' said Crook airily. 'But—never heard of the green-eyed monster? Mind you, I'd say there were faults on both sides. Mothers should share out their affections as scrupulously as if they were rations in war time. Only way to stop jealousy. But, being human, they never do. And here was the old lady making no secret of the fact that if her daughter and Miss Field were both drowning and she could only save one, her money would be on the girl. That's a bitter dose for any daughter to swallow.'

Miles said thoughtfully, 'You could never bring a case against her and hope to substantiate it. We've got Barbara's word that she may have pushed the bell away when she was hunting for the drops. . . .'

'Mrs Calmady's buried. No one wants to dig up a corpse. Pretty safe, I should think'—here he glanced across to Menzies —'to say nothing more will be done here unless Miss Calmady starts a slander campaign. No harm dropping her a hint in due course as to how the land lies,' he added dryly.

'I'd like to think you were wrong,' said Miles, 'but I have to admit it seems the only possible explanation. I never believed

Barbara was involved, any more than I believe she was responsible for Miss Carter's death.'

Barbara sent him a grateful glance; Crane looked troubled; Menzies looked at Crook. He was sitting humped in his chair like one of those outsize Toby jugs you buy at *ersatz* antique shops.

'What gives, Crook?' he murmured, adopting the lawyer's own technique.

Crook heaved a deep sigh. 'No sense doing any more covering up,' he said. 'There's been too much of that in this case already. I never did believe Miss Hurst gave old Mrs C her quietus. But Miss Carter's another matter. And in that case, Calmady, you lose your bet.'

If someone had flung open the door and held up the head of Medusa, compelling them all to look and thereby be turned to stone, the stillness within the room could not have been more complete. The expressions on the faces of his audience were fixed as in a photograph. For a minute no one spoke. On the sofa Julie made a faint movement, then sank back into unconsciousness. Philip Crane moved, as though that broke the spell, and went over to her side. He looked at Barbara as he went past, but she was staring at the ground, her face the colour of ashes. Crane stooped over the unconscious woman, touched her wrist, straightened himself.

'For a defence lawyer you strike me as being a bit defeatist,' he remarked coolly. 'And remember, statement without proof doesn't mean a thing in a court of law. And you'd never prove it.'

'Meaning that you believe it?' Miles's eyes flashed a chill blue fire.

'I mean that I've never been in any doubt. And if anyone quotes me I shall perjure myself to high Heaven. But after the inquest Barbara admitted to me that she had given Miss Carter the overdose.'

His eyes defied them all.

'Barbara,' he said, 'my offer's still open. Will you marry me?'

'Knowing what she's done?' exclaimed Miles, shocked.

'We don't know yet,' put in Menzies, his voice as dry as a November leaf. 'Crane says Miss Hurst told him, Crook says he knows it's true. . . . Perhaps you'd go one step farther and tell us why you're so sure,' he added in inimical tones.

'I've gone round and round the case like a dormouse round its wheel,' Crook acknowledged. 'I've gone up and down, and I've arranged the bits of evidence in every possible way and it all adds up to the same thing. There's no other explanation that fits the facts. You may as well start accepting the truth, because the Angel Gabriel couldn't change it. She gave the old lady the poison—poor girl.' He turned to Barbara. 'Don't you remember anything, even now?'

Barbara looked as though she had been felled by Jove's thunderbolt. If she even heard Crook's appeal she made no sign. Crane said, crossing to her side, 'Don't say anything, Barbara. This isn't a police case, and I'm sorry you ever started fresh inquiries. You'd have lived it down, we were going to settle in a different part of the country where Miss Carter wouldn't even be a name. But, however perspicacious Crook may be, he can't offer any proof. And in any case,' he added belligerently, turning towards Crook, 'I thought you were supposed to be acting for Barbara.'

'It won't help her at this stage to conceal the facts,' returned Crook wooden-faced and stubborn.

Barbara spoke. 'How could I have done it?' she whispered. 'How could I?'

'Yes,' said Miles. 'How could you? An old woman, at your mercy. . . . You, Barbara!'

'There are tensions in the human mind that transcend reason,' Crane told him sharply. 'Reason's like a piece of elastic. You can stretch it so far, but if you put too much pressure on it it will snap. Barbara had had a very difficult time, she was young, she had no one but myself, outside the household, to whom to turn, she had her plans and—I think I may say this for both of us—she was very much in love, as indeed I was myself. At this stage, when she was exhausted and naturally keyed up by the situation, Miss Carter, for no reason I have ever been able to understand, decides to send for her lawyer. Obviously she can

have had but one aim in doing this. Whether she explained to
Barbara what she intended to do or not I can't swear, but at
the inquest she assured us that she knew nothing of Miss
Carter's intentions. There was the situation. Barbara wasn't as
fortunate as many of us, she had had no home life, she had
worked very hard for the old lady, she was looking forward to
the first true security she had ever known, and at this moment
she saw the prospect of it being snatched out of her grasp. It
was too much for her reason. . . .'

'And you're advancing that as an excuse for murder?' Miles's
voice was cold with shock.

Crane whirled round upon him. 'Not an excuse, but an
explanation. I don't suppose you've ever found yourself in a
similar position. Barbara,' he turned back to the girl, 'you'd do
well to accept my offer. Remember, this isn't between the two
of us any longer, and things leak out, no matter how careful the
precautions you take. A husband can't be brought up to give
evidence against his wife, and I'm the only other person in the
picture.'

'Is Crook prepared to substantiate his claim?' demanded
Menzies.

'I've told you, you can't arrange the facts any other way. It's
like putting furniture in a slip room. You have to range it
against the wall, because there ain't the floor space for any
fancy patterns.'

'Barbara,' said Menzies clearly, 'don't let yourself be rushed.
You've broken off your engagement with Crane once. No doubt
you had your reasons. You may not know what those reasons
were but they may still hold good. He's not the only arrow in
your quiver. . . .'

'Little Dan Cupid,' murmured Crook. 'What a boy! You
can't keep him out, can you?'

Miles found his voice again. 'Doesn't it mean a thing to any
of you that this girl murdered Miss Carter?'

'Who says so?' demanded Crook quick as light. 'I never said
anything about murder. I just said she gave the old lady the
fatal dose. If you want to pin a murder label on anyone look
towards the chap who supplied the poison.'

And taking a step forward he laid his hand on Philip Crane's arm.

A sleepy bee buzzed on the pane; it was a soothing sound, but to the ears of the listeners in that small enclosed space it was as loud as the humming of an aeroplane. Buzz-zz-zz. It walked a few steps up the glass, slid down and started again. Barbara had sunk back as though she would join Julie in her indifferent state. Miles stared, incredulous, Menzies was impassive, but Crook, glancing at him, thought, 'I wouldn't care to be that chap's enemy. It 'ud be wrestle, gouge and rabbit-punch and no holds barred.' Julie created a diversion by uttering a long moaning sound and opening her eyes.

She stared vaguely about her, a creature newly released from sleep, not yet accepting her environs. That bland vacant gaze went from Miles to Menzies, from Menzies to Crane, by-passed Crook (you wouldn't have thought it could be done but Julie did it) and came to rest on Barbara's apparently lifeless face. Sudden intelligence lit the brown eyes.

'Has she killed herself?' demanded Julie. 'She tried to kill me, you know. The knife.' Then she seemed to recognise Miles. 'Why did you follow me here?'

'I wanted to make sure you didn't do Barbara any harm,' he retorted with unexpected brutality.

If he had wanted to arouse her he could have found no better way.

'Always Barbara,' she cried furiously. 'Do you know what she did?' She fixed her angry eyes on Mr Crook. 'I thought I told you I didn't want to see you again.'

Crook caught the conversational ball and biffed it back over the net without a second's hesitation.

'This happens to be Miss Hurst's flat—had you forgotten?— and I'm here by invitation. Investigatin' a couple of murders, if you're curious,' he added chattily.

'I'm sure you're disappointed it isn't three,' she fired at him.

'Don't count your chickens,' Crook warned her, and then Crane broke in, speaking in a very quiet, tense voice: 'Would you care to explain what you've just said?'

'Easy enough,' replied Crook. 'You provided the poison that

polished off the old lady. Is that simple enough for you?'

'Well, but we knew that all along,' Miles Calmady protested. 'It was established from the beginning that she had died of an overdose of sleeping-tablets. We knew the tablets came from Crane's dispensary. You can't hang a murder charge on him on that account.'

'No?' murmured Crook. 'You'd be surprised.'

'We're waiting,' Crane offered.

Crook knew, if the others didn't, that innocent men are never so calm as this. Innocence begets a healthy indignation in the face of accusation, an indignation that sometimes expresses itself in a determined attempt to cleave the adversary from crown to chine.

'Thinking of bringing an action, Doc?' he suggested. 'Forget it! You don't want a life sentence any more than the next man, and I don't blame you. Even if they couldn't bring a true bill against you, it wouldn't do you much good to find your patients scuttling off to get their names on some other fellow's panel. Considerin' how much grumbling chaps do while they are alive, it's astonishin' how few of 'em really do want to go before their time. Now,' he added, 'let's all sit around and be cosy. That's right, Menzies, you look after my client the way you're doing at this minute, Calmady, keep an eye on your lady friend, and the doctor 'ull have to play lady for me. Come to that, he's as tricky as any pair of janes I ever had to deal with.'

For himself, he leaned against the diminutive modern mantel-piece, looking like a pig baron. Crane thrust his hands in his pockets and glanced warily about him.

'There was something said earlier about a jigsaw puzzle,' explained Crook, 'to the effect that there's times when it's all done bar one piece, and there's one vacant space, but the piece don't fit into the space. So what you have to do is go over the pattern and see where you've jammed in the wrong bit. Same like it was here. Y'see, it was obvious to a blind man that the trouble started with the letters that arrived that morning. Mean to say, there'd been no question of sending for a lawyer, Miss Hurst here hadn't intended to go out on a wild-goose chase after flimflams nobody wanted, and—here's the point—nobody expected the doctor to call. He'd been there the previous day and he'd posted the prescription, so—what gives? Nobody had used the telephone that morning, and there hadn't been any incoming calls. That drove me back to the letters. One from nephew saying he's coming along with some documents. One from Miss Thingmajigg, who's in bed with a temperature, one from the gas company, an advertisement, and a prescription. Count out the nephew, count out Pussy in her basket. Not much to be made of the gas foreman and even less of the advertisement. Which leaves the prescription.'

Miles looked up. 'You mean the prescription was at fault and that that accounts for Miss Carter taking an overdose? And Crane hadn't the nerve to come forward and admit it?'

'You're ridin' in front of the hounds,' Crook told him. 'You're forgetting his visit to the house that morning.'

'In connection with the prescription?'

'Yes,' agreed Crook reflectively. 'You could say it was in connection with the prescription. D'you know what struck me as funny? That though Crane didn't come round till about 11 o'clock, and the prescription was urgent enough to be posted instead of bein' brought round on his next visiting day, *it wasn't taken to the chemist till after lunch*. And yet Miss Hurst went out that morning, and actually passed the chemist's shop. So why not drop it in? Well, there's only one answer I can think of, and that is that Miss Carter hadn't got it when Miss Hurst left the flat.'

'You're like a cat that always uses the longest way to come home,' interrupted Crane contemptuously. 'I found in the morning that I'd sent Miss Carter the wrong prescription—it was a perfectly harmless headache mixture she'd had the previous year and wanted again for emergencies—so I came round to bring the right one.'

'Tell me this,' said Crook. 'How did you discover it was the wrong prescription?'

'Because I'd sent a second prescription to another patient and she rang up to tell me it was the wrong one. So I realised, of course, what had happened. I'd written out the prescriptions, been interrupted—the telephone or something, I don't recall precisely what—and accidentally mailed them to the wrong people. Neither of them was mortal. . . .'

'No?' murmured Crook. 'But someone died just the same. How come your other patient knew she had the wrong one?'

'It's customary to write a patient's name on a prescription,' Crane pointed out.

'So, of course, Miss Carter would know, too, that she had somebody else's dope?'

'Presumably.'

'And yet she don't ring through and tell you there's been a mistake, and will you please put it right? And you, when you hear from your lady friend, you don't ring Miss Carter's house and say, "There's been a bit of a blunder, don't get that prescription made up, I'll send the right one round." No, you put on your best bib and tucker and come beetlin' round in person, though it's not your rightful day. What's more, Miss Carter knew you were coming.'

'How do you make that out?' demanded Crane.

'The way she sent Miss Hurst off the premises to waste good bawbees. There are old ladies who like to chuck their money about, but Miss C was never one of them, and knowing how close she was to the Pearly Gates there wasn't much reason for her to go cluttering herself up with stuff she'd never use. All the same, she sends Miss Hurst out, knowing Crane will call.'

'You're taking a good deal for granted,' objected Miles uneasily. 'How did she know?'

'Because she knew he'd come in for the enclosure he'd put in the wrong envelope.'

'The prescription?' Miles still sounded puzzled.

'Who says it was a prescription? Oh, Dr Crane, yes. But he hasn't explained why in the middle of a busy morning he came round to collect a prescription or why he stayed as long as he did. It don't explain Miss Carter sending her companion out, and it don't explain why there wasn't any to-ing and fro-ing on the telephone in that connection. No, no, you take my word for it, what Crane came round for was something about as harmless as dynamite; and he came because the lady to whom the enclosure was addressed had got him on the line and warned him the fat was in the fire and unless he was lucky the whole house was likely to go up. Of course,' he turned to Crane, 'you must have hoped Miss Carter was the kind of lady that wouldn't read a letter that wasn't meant for her, but if you really thought that you missed out for once, didn't you? Because she hadn't only read it, she meant to act on it—as is proved by her getting Wotton to ring Menzies here. And it's a point that she didn't wait for Barbara to do it. "Don't tell her I've sent for him," she told Wotton. "I've been deceived all along the line." Who by? Not Carter. You can't be deceived by someone you've never trusted from the start. Not Wotton, or it wouldn't be Wotton ringing Menzies's office. Barbara Hurst? But in that case why not give the girl the key of the street right away? No, that bit about experience being wasted if it don't teach you some sense could only apply to Crane.'

The doctor here interposed sarcastically, 'You should really be writing pot boilers, Crook. You'd make quite a packet out of them.'

Crook replied, unemotionally, that he did very nicely, thank you, Jack, the way it was, and went on, 'As a girl, Miss Carter had been led up the garden path by a suitor who was more interested in what she had than what she was, and I fancy that's what she had in mind. She didn't mean Barbara to go the same way. History has a trick of repeating itself, they tell me.'

'And she informed me that she was going to disinherit Barbara sooner than let her marry me? Is that what you're asking us to believe?'

'It don't matter a pin either way,' Crook assured him, 'seeing you're no slouch and can tell a hawk from a handsaw with the best of us. It was neat of you to ask for 24 hours' grace—or 48 maybe. . . .'

'Grace?'

'Well, why didn't she tell the little girl as soon as she came in? She didn't; and she didn't mean her to know about Menzies coming. I suppose she wanted to save her face as much as possible. Or maybe you said, "Keep your mouth shut and I swear I'll break it off, but don't let Barbara know the facts."

The old lady 'ud agree, I'm sure. Once you knew the nine thousand had taken wings there wouldn't be any more talk of wedding-bells. And you wouldn't care what she meant to do, because you were going to see to it she didn't get the chance of cutting your girl out or doing anything else.'

'That amounts to a tacit accusation that I poisoned her?' Crane pointed out levelly.

'So it does,' Crook agreed, with all the heartiness in the world.

'I never heard anything so preposterous. Mind you, if you could show I'd doped the old lady's drink or somehow given her a fatal dose when I was a mile away, then you might have a case, but when I left the flat the milk hadn't even been poured out.'

'What's the milk got to do with it?'

'I beg your pardon,' said Crane elaborately. 'I thought you were going to prove that the additional tablets were put in the glass or cup before it reached Miss Carter's bedside.'

'What additional tablets?' Crook's expression was as wooden as a monkey on a stick.

Crane was all at sea now. 'The jury found that Miss Carter had taken four or five tablets instead of her customary two. . . .'

'That's not what I read,' said Crook. 'It said the poison was equivalent to the contents of four or five of her usual sleeping-pills, quite a different pair of dancing-pumps.'

Menzies was the first to get there. 'Good heavens, Crook, do you mean there's nothing to show that the whole dose wasn't administered in the two tablets Miss Hurst admittedly gave her?'

'If anyone present has any other explanation, I'm open to suggestions,' Crook offered.

'Look,' expostulated Crane. 'The phial of tablets was taken into custody by the police. I never had a chance of handling them, and they were shown to be of the normal strength. What's your answer to that?'

'You say you never had a chance of handling them, but what you mean is you never handled them after Miss Carter was found dead. But—who supplied 'em in the first place?'

'I did, of course, but . . .'

'And when? That's the crux of the situation.'

'The night before, when Miss Hurst rang me up to say the original phial was missing.'

'And that's something else no one's explained, how it came to be missing, I mean.'

'You can hardly hold me responsible for that. It was seen by Major Carter during the afternoon, some hours after my visit.'

'Was it?' questioned Crook. 'I talked to the gallant major myself, and all he's prepared to admit in the witness-box it that he saw a phial he assumed to be the sleeping-tablets, on a bed-table. But a chap like that wouldn't know the difference between sleeping-tablets in a tube and any other sort of dope—digestion pills or what-have-you. And Miss Carter had various mixtures, as most old people do. No, I don't think you can flunk out on that. The fact remains that the pills were there that morning when you called and they couldn't be found that night.'

'I take it you're suggesting Crane carried them off with him,' put in Miles. 'What was the idea of that?'

'So that he could substitute another phial when the loss of this one was discovered. No, don't give me the one about the pills being all Sir Garnet when they were examined by the police. Of course they were, all that were left of them. Haven't you got there yet? *Only the two top pills were important.* They were the ones that would be given to the old lady that night. They were in a tube, remember, and when you're taking tablets of any sort out of a tube you take them as they come. So—it's only the two top ones, that Miss Carter took in her drink that evening, that matter. And my case is that there was enough of the dope in those two pills to send old Miss C to Kingdom Come. Yes, of course that's how it was. You meant to have that £9000, come what may. And you were getting a very pretty girl thrown in, with no relations to make trouble, and she was daft enough to let you have the money for this practice or any other cause you put before her. A sensible girl in love is as rare as a unicorn, and though I've been about a good deal that's something I've never set eyes on yet. Well, everything's set for a happy ending for you at least, when you put up a black. You mixed two envelopes, and you knew at once the fat was in the fire. This lady—this Mrs Sharp——'

'What's that? Who told you her name?' Amazement jerked the words from Crane's lips.

'I'm coming to that. She had something on you, hadn't she? And she wrote asking for—what? Money? A wedding ring? It don't signify. Anyhow you wrote, telling her, I dare say, that you were expecting a nice little legacy shortly, just be patient a little longer and we can all splash in the gravy. Oh, I don't say that was the way you put it, but whatever it was it was enough to open Miss Carter's eyes. As I said, you worked fast. I don't say you had murder in mind when you rang the bell of the flat, but it's my experience that murder's not often a flash-in-the-pan affair. I mean, fellows are prepared to kill if the occasion arises, even if they don't know it themselves. So you resolved to put out the old lady's light. But how? There was one obvious way and that was by an overdose. Really, that notion was handed to you on a plate. Only how were you going to persuade her to take a double draught? You couldn't risk coming back that evening and you hadn't an accomplice, couldn't have in the circumstances. The notion of substituting fatal pills for the harmless ones must have come to you while she was talking, and I'll say this for you, you don't waste any time. You knew the old lady had to have her pills, you knew the loss wouldn't be discovered till all the chemists were shut—that was important— so the prescription couldn't be made up before the next day. That meant Miss Hurst would have to telephone to you. You have your own dispensary, don't you? And the pills would be ready waiting for the call. Well, you get it, round come the pills and quite innocently your young lady hands a cup of cold pizen to old Miss Carter. You know you'll be telephoned the minute she's found, that is, the next morning. All you have to do is come round and shake your head and say, "Heart failure, very sad but none of us lives for ever, and she'd had a good run for her money, so dry your eyes, sugar, and get ready for wedding bells." I wouldn't put it past you to say it was what she'd have wished. Right, honey?'

Barbara was shaking and so pale Miles was frightened for her. Menzies had listened like a stone.

'I don't know,' whispered Barbara. 'Mr Crook, there's something that would give us a clue. If I could recognise what it was, something that was wrong. If only I could remember. . . .'

'Don't strain yourself, sugar. It'll come back. Of course, Crane here couldn't know that two fool drivers were going to get mixed up in his neighbourhood and he was going to be called out for first aid. He wouldn't dare refuse to go—he'd have been on the BMA mat if he had—so all he could hope was that that little job would be tied up before the inevitable telephone call came through. And this was one time when prayer wasn't answered. By the time you could cut loose it was too late, a whole lot too late. I'll say you were in a stew when you got back and couldn't be sure if the call had come through or not, and you couldn't ring the flat, because it might look as though you were expecting bad news—well, news anyway. Still, even when you knew what had happened and Martin had refused the certificate, you still held some cards. The missing phial, for instance, because the suggestion was that there hadn't been enough in that to constitute a fatal dose, so you put in for reinforcements.' He was speaking to Barbara now. 'I bet he was full of sympathy when he saw which way the wind was blowing. Did he renew his offer of marriage by any chance?'

Barbara's face looked ghastly in the bright sunlight. 'Mr Crook, that's it. He didn't say anything till after the inquest. . . .'

'Well, of course not,' said Crook sensibly. 'Murderers can't profit from their crimes, you know, and he had to be sure of the nine thousand. But afterwards . . .'

'He said, "Thank God, Barbara, you were able to swing it. I've been on tenterhooks. . . ." '

'I'll say,' put in Crook in heartfelt tones.

' "Now you're in the clear there's nothing to stop us. We can be married in twenty-four hours, once we've given notice to the registrar." '

'I said, "But what's the hurry?" and he said, "You don't know much about the police. The fact that the coroner's jury brought in what's virtually an open verdict doesn't mean they won't go on with their inquiries. Husbands and wives can't be called on to give evidence against each other . . ." I said, "But, Philip, you can't believe I really did it," and he said, "It's one of those mysteries for which sensible people don't demand explanations. I suppose it's possible she took the extra tablets herself . . ." But he didn't believe it and nor did I. She wouldn't do that just when she'd sent for Mr Menzies. The only other explanation was that I'd made a muddle and given her a double dose, only— how could I do that accidentally? I'd been giving her these tablets for months. No, it seemed to me he was sure I was guilty and—it didn't matter. But that doesn't make sense, Mr Crook. You couldn't want to marry a murderess. Why, it could happen again. You'd be bound to think of that. And anyway, I couldn't get married within twenty-four hours of her funeral. I said, "You have to call banns, don't you, before you can get married?" And he said, "Not if it's by licence. You have to notify the registrar, of course. and then you can get tied up at twenty-four hours' notice. And I gave notice some time ago." That's when I began to realise something was . . .'

'Fishy?' suggested Crook.

'Why?' asked Miles flatly.

'Because it was understood that there was to be no talk of marriage until after Miss Carter didn't need me any more. Oh, I know what you're thinking,' she cried, meeting Julie's venomous glance, 'you think it was because I didn't get the money unless I was in her service at the time of her death, but it wasn't that at all. I couldn't have left her in any circumstances so long as she needed me. Why, she was the first "family" I'd ever had. So—what possessed him to notify the registrar of our marriage *unless he knew she was going to die?* Mr Crook, I thought and thought, but I couldn't find any other answer at all. And how could he know, how could he . . . ?'

'Unless he'd done a bit of engineering himself. Well, Crane, how could you?' He turned back to Barbara. 'Happen to know what precise day your gentleman friend gave notice to the registrar?'

Barbara's face was twisted with distress. 'That was just it, Mr Crook. It was the day before she died, and there'd never been any question that she might die suddenly. He knew, Mr Crook, he must have known. And then I got to thinking about that fatal dose. You see, I knew I must have given her the poison, there wasn't anyone else, and yet I knew she'd only had two tablets. So it was obvious that I must have given her the fatal dose. And then I understood—everything cleared up like a cloud suddenly passing off the face of the sun, and I saw how it must have been; though I didn't know why, except, of course, that she must have meant to change her will. Wotton and Major Carter had gone to the funeral, Philip said he'd be coming along later, but I couldn't see him, Mr Crook, I couldn't see him. I didn't want to see anyone, just wanted to get away, even from myself. That's when I packed the case—I suppose that's why I didn't take anything personal that would identify me to myself. I just launched off into the blue, as it were, didn't book a room or anything, and on the journey the thing I'd been wishing for happened, I lost even myself. I turned into Barbara Field, and if Mr Menzies hadn't turned up, I might never have got back.'

'A very interesting story,' said Crane cordially. 'It would be better, of course, if you could prove a word of it.'

'Who says she can't?' inquired Crook calmly, taking the girl's shaking hands between his own, and patting them; it was rather like being patted by a panther. 'You might like to explain putting your names down for the Matrimonial Stakes just when you did. And, of course, there's still the dark horse, the lady who started all the trouble.'

'In a minute you're going to tell us how you know her name and address.'

'Did you ever think how easy it is for a chap to ring through to the exchange and explain he's a doctor and he's trying to trace a number, a trunk call, that got through to him on such-and-such a day, in this case the 14th, the same day as you went to see the registrar, Crane?'

'I haven't the least idea what you're driving at,' said the doctor, with obvious truth.

'I'll tell you. It bothered me a bit why you should wait till 11 o'clock to go round and collect your letter. I mean, your lady-friend either rises very late or lives a long way off. She'd get in touch the minute she realised the bloomer you'd made, and yet it's the middle of the morning before you go traipsing round to Miss Carter's flat. So it seemed likely to me she only got it on the second post, which would mean it must be a trunk call. So, as I say, I got on to the young lady at the exchange with a sob-sister yarn about bein' a doctor and tryin' to trace a next-of-kin who'd rung me on the 14th and whose number I'd mislaid. Matter of life and death, I said, could she possibly trace the call? And when she did I got an inquiry or so out. You'd known the lady rather well at one time, hadn't you? And it wasn't going to be her fault if you didn't know her ever better. I take it you never mentioned to *her* you were running for the Matrimonial Stakes? Not that I blame you; I'd as soon tangle up with a lady asp myself.'

'Is that the strength of your case?' demanded Crane scornfully. 'Why, you haven't even got the letter in question.'

'We've got the lady, though,' said Crook, 'and she won't mind going into the box. You'll have to change the name on that marriage notice of yours, won't you?'

Crane looked around him, but he might as easily have looked for softening in the pillars of Stonehenge as in those icy faces.

He summoned up his bravado and demanded, 'Well, what's the next move? I warn you, if you so much as start a whispering campaign against me I'll bring an action for slander, and I hardly think, Barbara, my dear, you'd do well to court any more publicity. If you take my advice . . .'

'She don't have to,' said Crook woodenly. 'She's got her own man of affairs now.'

In that instant Crane must have seen that everything was lost—the money, the girl, reputation, hope, the future. A wave of sheer hatred shook him as though he were battling in a driving gale.

'You don't lose much time, do you?' he suggested, turning to Barbara, 'Chuck yourself first at my head, and then . . .'

He got no farther. Menzies took a quick step across the room and struck him in the face. Crane was so much surprised that he fell down and Menzies flung himself upon him. With difficulty Crook prised him free.

'Ain't two bodies enough for you?' he demanded. 'They are for me. Providence only gave me two hands.'

Julie let out a wild scream and was instantly gagged by her cousin. The scene was pandemonium. It was abruptly broken up by the appearance of Hill, who let himself in with the pass-key.

'What the 'ell's going on 'ere?' he demanded furiously. 'Anyone 'ud think it was a murder.'

'Anyone,' agreed Crook politely, 'might be right.'

EPILOGUE

'I'll say one thing for you, Crook,' remarked Menzies hand-somely, a day or two later. 'You don't mind sticking your neck out. How much of a case had you really got against Crane?'

'You're mixing me up with the police,' said Crook placidly. 'Mind you, I know a private citizen can bring a murder charge, but even if you're right about me sticking out my neck I don't want it busted, any more than anyone else. Case? Well, there's no doubt in my mind he did it, and I fancy if it came to a court the jury might think the same. Still, no one ever saw him take the phial, and the affair could be made to smell of collusion. Not that he'd want this Mrs Sharp to go into the witness-box. She's definitely one of Nature's mistakes, five years older than Crane and been through the divorce courts already. Of course, what she was out for was a wedding ring; she couldn't expect to get much in cash from a young GP. And he was ambitious and Barbara Hurst was a great chance for him, especially as she seems to have fallen for him in a big way. Still,' he put a com-forting hand on his companion's arm. 'She'll get over it, pal. With a bit of help from you, I dare say. Mind you,' he went on, harking back to his former subject, 'if Crane hadn't tried to foist the crime on the girl I could almost have felt sorry for him. I wouldn't want my worst enemy to marry that Mrs Sharp, and the way Miss Carter was playing it, it looked as though he was goin' to be driven into her arms. Come to think of it, what could he do to quiet the old girl except murder her? By the way,' he went on, 'where have you left the little girl to-night? Not on her lonesome surely? She seems to be more or less your responsibility now.'

182

'She's staying with my mother *pro tem*,' Menzies explained. 'I didn't care for the idea of her being in that flat with a possible murderer—two possible murderers, rather—on the loose. I must say I don't envy Calmady with that lunatic cousin tied round his neck. Give me a dead albatross every time.'

'Remember the war?' said Crook. 'How there were chaps known as bomb-attractors or whatever the right phrase may be? Wherever they went the bombs followed them. Barbara Hurst went to Miss Carter and she died, not from natural causes; ditto Mrs Calmady. You ain't afraid you might find yourself up against a third brick wall?'

'I'll chance it,' said Menzies.

But if there was any truth in the idea that things go by threes, Menzies was cleared a day or two later by a small paragraph in the evening paper to the effect that a laundry van had come into collision with a motor-car at a cross-roads and the driver of the car had received fatal injuries. His name? Philip Crane, doctor, aged 29, of Beeston Way, London.

'Taking his own way out?' wondered Menzies, for there had been whispers of a possible reopening of the Carter case. But Crook said you had to give the chap the benefit of the doubt and anyone could have an accident and one man's meat, etc., and here was a death the most malicious couldn't try and pin on Barbara Hurst. 'Anyway,' he added, 'I doubt if anyone goes into mourning for him.'

When Mr and Mrs Robert Menzies returned from their honeymoon about two months later, they were met at the airport by a large ancient Rolls of a vivid yellow shade, driven by a man who, in the opinion of a female spectator, looked more like a gorilla than any human being should dare to look. He drove his passengers back to London, and insisted on taking them out to a celebration dinner at a place neither had ever heard of, but where Crook was evidently *persona grata* and where the food might even have won a commendation from Lucullus himself.

During the meal he tied up the loose ends for them.

'Julie Calmady is in one of these posh nursing-homes that are really mental prisons in disguise. Thinks she's the Queen of Sheba or someone, probably happier than she's been for years. They'll never try and hang anything on her and, on the other hand, I doubt if she ever gets away. Miles has got the house up for sale and has settled in a small one about a mile distant, still a bachelor, but that won't last. Chap hasn't got the staying power. It's just a question of which of the besieging dames can run the fastest. As for Crane, well, you know about him. And quite apart from Miss Carter, sugar, you were well out of that. I've met his sort before. Twenty-four hours after marriage he suggests you both make a will, and before you've got accustomed to signing your cheques with your new name, it's a case of The angels in Heaven are singing to-day, *Here's Johnnie, here's Johnnie, here's Johnnie!* Whereas this way'—he put a hand on Menzies's shoulder and almost broke it—'you've settled for the real McCoy. Always look for a chap with red hair, sugar, they never let you down.'